The Triple Crown of Jewel Theft

J.A. DEVEREAUX

Book Covers and Title Page by Jeffrey Kosh Graphics
    (Contracted/Purchased by J. A. Devereaux and used with permission)
Original Front Cover Photo © Saveliev Dmytro/Shutterstock.com
    (Purchased by J. A. Devereaux and used with permission)
    Edited and reformatted by Jeffrey Kosh, Jeffrey Kosh Graphics
Author Pictures by Jessii Terra Photos
    (Contracted/Purchased by J. A. Devereaux and used with permission)

A

Cunning
Thief
Books

Publication

ISBN- 9781670043504

The Triple Crown of Jewel Theft is a work of fiction. References to real events, establishments, organizations, or locales are used only to provide a sense of authenticity and are used fictitiously. All other names, characters, and incidents are the product of the author's imagination. Any resemblance to actual events, places, or persons—living, dead, or other fictional characters—is unintended and/or coincidental.

The *Thief à la Femme* Series:

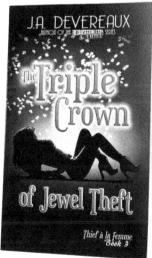

Funny, romantic and mysterious! And that's just the main character!

J.A. Devereaux has done it again. What a great start to a new series. I literally had to slow down my reading so I could better enjoy the story line. And then, just as I get ready to flip the page for a new chapter...there isn't one. Disappointment and anticipation at the same time! This new series seems to have it all: Humor, sexy romance (but in good taste) and of course the plot thickens with mystery!

This new series will satisfy fans looking for drama

Exceeded my expectations, which were high to begin with based on the author's previous work. This new series will satisfy fans looking for drama, suspense, thrills, conflict, fun and even sensuality. I highly recommend fans of any of the above genres pick up a copy of this book!

Robin [(s) of the] Hood...ladies that rule!

Love the new series book 1...I am very excited to get book 2. Definitely great ending...you left us hanging! I am ordering some books for gifts to my friends. I read the first series and I can't wait to read this series.

Female Super Thief!

Once again, a very well written tome. Very compelling main character, a female Super thief. Tense plot line with a touch of romance. Heroine is almost unbelievable. Final chapter is left as a cliffhanger. Good hook, J.A.!

Female Thief

I am so loving this new series and very anxious to read the next. J.A. Devereaux is giving us another well-written series. The characters seem so realistic. Of course, that cliffhanger at the end is going to keep me wondering what is next. So many questions I'm sure will be answered in the upcoming books.

Born to Steal ... of course she is!

Born to steal is fast-paced action with a modern female version of Robin Hood. I read it in three sittings. Although I didn't feel I knew Rayla quite as well as I knew Gregg from her earlier Thief books, I have no doubt J. A. Devereaux will expand Rayla's character as well as her exploits as this series progresses. Sign me up for Book 2!

WordPress Review

The delightful second book of J.A. Devereaux's new series

J.A. Devereaux's thief.con: (Thief a la Femme Book 2) is a delightful follow up to Book 1. Once again, she does an outstanding job describing everything, the characters, the locals, the heists. I really hope to read a lot more about Rayla and Luke in the future. Books and books worth.

Riveting…

As I reread book 1 in this series, I was astonished to find I was actually a participant. At least that's what if felt like as I read. JA has a writing style that brings you right into the story line. But book 2? What a riveting read complete with JA's unique twists and turns. As I read page after page, I wanted to see where the story leads and yet hated to think it would be finished. And, I even had the nerve to think I had it figured out before the ending…Boy, was I wrong!!! And really glad I was! This series should speak to all age groups and those who like romance and heists.

Thank you, JA, for another great read.

Fantastic Story!

I had a hard time putting this down. This author is such a good writer. If you haven't read any of her books (including her Requisition For: A Thief series) I recommend you start now. Loved the characters the female Thief and the FBI agent. I can't wait to read more of their continuing story and more of the other characters. Thanks for writing such a fantastic story!

Great continuation of the story!
The plot was intricate, but easy to follow. The thief is human and believable. Great read! kept me interested far too long, trying to figure out what was happening! Devereaux is a compelling writer. Keep up the Great work!

Thieves
I loved these books! I raced through 1 and 2 and was so disappointed when there wasn't a third! How about remedying that please!

She's a burglar and an author.
NO ONE writes about or describes a heist better than J.A. Devereaux! Her love of storytelling is evident in all of her books, her research is meticulous, and her love of burglary is irresistible. Do yourself a favor and pick up both series—this one and her Requisition For: A Thief series.

Love the Characters!
Great story line and vivid characters. Enjoyed reading this book and all the other books by this author. This is the second series by this author. First series (Requisition For: A Thief) was spot on as well. I always feel good at the end of her books...and want more.

The REQISITION FOR: A THIEF Series
[Those *Other* Books by J. A. Devereaux]

Watch for

Coming Fall 2020

The Triple Crown
of Jewel Theft

Thief à la Femme
Book 3

J. A. DEVEREAUX

Cunning
Thief
Books

For Barb and Deb

1

"PUT IT BACK," Luke whispered, his hushed tone and demeanor reminiscent of a father concerned for his child's wayward ways.

Rayla laughed. Not because her FBI boyfriend wanted her to return the article she'd stolen, but specifically because of the way he'd stated his request—as more of a command. But, besides that, him telling her to "put it back," was just plain humorous. As much as she loved him, Special Agent Luke Keltry tended to be somewhat uncompromising when it came to her thieving vocation.

Because that's what she was.

A thief.

And an exceptionally good one. Everyone she knew, as well as countless news headlines, substantiated that claim.

Luke knew all about her yet had still pursued her with notably more fervor than he had his quest to arrest her. In truth, her being the infamous *Thief à la Femme*, as well as a member of the notorious thieving sisterhood known as "Robin(s) of the Hood" made up a huge part of his attraction for her—a pertinent detail she'd known from the start of their relationship. Similarly, her amorous attraction for him included the forbidden element of him being an FBI agent. *In love with a fed. Talk about complicated...*

The fact she'd lifted the watch off Luke's former girlfriend's wrist at his best friend's wedding—where Luke was Josh's best man and the clueless former girlfriend was maid of honor—might have something to do with his concern. But she

1

didn't think so. She knew Luke well enough at this point, almost three months into their relationship, to recognize the spark of admiration he held for her larcenous abilities flickering in his large, maple-syrup-colored eyes.

"You were right," Rayla said. "She *is* a bitch. How long did you date her? I knew she was all wrong for you the moment I met her."

Luke failed in his attempt to keep his features stern and cracked an unwilling smile. "Don't deflect. You lifted that watch without her knowing, and she still hasn't missed it. Now I want to see if you're good enough to put it back the same way."

He was baiting her, using psychological BS to coax her into returning the watch under the guise of proving her talents, but she played along, her lips parting with mock incredulity if not outright hilarity. "You must be kidding. You wouldn't have known I lifted it, either, if I hadn't showed it to you." With that nugget of truth, she held up *his* watch.

His priceless look of surprise coupled with his hand robotically checking his wrist. He didn't reprove her again, though. She'd impressed him.

"Let's go, hotshot," he reiterated, snatching his watch from her grasp. "Show me your best reverse pull."

"I could show you my worst and get the job done without you or her seeing me do it."

Luke rewarded her confidence with a pinch-lipped grin. "Then do it, already."

"You're such a spoilsport," she said with a cocky smirk. Nevertheless, a few minutes later, Amber was again wearing her pricey Rolex, having been none the wiser for its temporary disappearance. Rayla had returned the timepiece while Luke's ex bent to retrieve her fallen clutch—the palm-size purse having been bumped from her grasp by another of Rayla's slick maneuvers—and she'd done it behind her back without so much as a glance in the woman's direction. Luke's honest admission he had not seen the reverse pull was an added perk, one which awarded her great satisfaction.

When she returned to his side, he escorted her through the French doors to the Arlington, Virginia banquet facility's twentieth-floor balcony. The birds'-eye-view of DC, lit up like Christmas decorations, took her breath away as did the early September evening's cool breeze, which caused goosebumps to erupt across her bare arms and shoulders. Luke removed his tux coat, wrapped it around her, and tugged her closer by its lapels until their lips met in a passionate kiss. She leaned in for more, but he pulled back.

"As much as I love watching you work, my best friend's wedding is not an appropriate venue for you to practice your pickpocketing skills while seeking to impress me, Rayla." His smile belied any possibility he might truly be upset with her as he tenderly swept a rogue strand of hair from her eyelashes. "You don't need to do that, anyway. You must be bored."

That was true, but she didn't want to throw a wet dishrag on her honey's one and only opportunity to spend time with his best friend since the FBI had relocated Luke to the west coast. Josh was a friend Luke had grown up with. They had even been stationed in the same FBI field office in DC for the first three years of Luke's blossoming career.

Her sexy and talented FBI beau would undoubtedly still be in DC, holding the second in command position within the first-ever High-End Theft Unit, if not for her. His desire to track her down, his desire *for her*, had led to his being in the right place at the right time. There, he had proven his exceptional capabilities as a top-rate HETU agent to the head of LA's FBI field office.

That smashingly successful audition brought about the Bureau director's decision to create a second HETU on the west coast and Luke being offered the supervisor position for the unit. It had been the perfect setup for the two of them to continue their off-the-Bureau's-radar affair—turning what had been a short fling into a promising long-term romance.

Her gaze found his and she tendered a demure smile. "Bored isn't the right term," she answered, scrunching her nose and lightly biting her lower lip. "Illegally excited is more accurate. I haven't seen this much bling in one room in quite a while. The temptation is getting to me."

Luke flashed his brilliantly white smile before sweeping her into his masculine embrace. "Then I'd better get you out of here as soon as possible. I can tell Josh is already suspicious of you. Things start going missing, you'll be the first he'll look to."

"You think he suspects you caught up with *Thief à la Femme*, are actually dating her, and aren't telling him?"

"He knew I was on your trail as a Robin(s) thief in California—even helped me find out which condo you were renting and the name you were using once you skipped on me in Santa Barbara. Then I got the new west coast HETU position, and I haven't said squat about the Robin(s) or *Thief à la Femme* in my few chats with him. I hoped he'd believe I was too busy with my new job, and my new girlfriend, to get back to pursuing my obsession with you ladies, but it makes sense he'd be wondering about it. Besides, you look exactly like I dreamed the infamous *Thief à la Femme* would, and Josh knows that."

"But that should help him believe I'm not her, shouldn't it? I mean it stands to reason you'd find another female with the physical traits you're so enamored with and he'd assume you've moved on."

"I'd think that, too, if I hadn't noticed him staring at you on more than a couple of occasions since we arrived this weekend, not to mention the interrogation-like, fact-finding conversations he's had with you. It's not your physical qualifications that have his radar up. You fit the precise, feisty profile of a top-notch thief to a T. Josh is a White-Collar

Division agent, which means he's worked on more than a few cases involving high-end thieves. He knows the type, and I'm pretty sure he's got you pegged. He's really good at his job."

Rayla snaked her fingers through his golden and blond layered locks and snuggled closer, laying her cheek against his rock-hard pecs and appreciating every gorgeous inch of him. "He's got nothing, Luke. He can't prove a thing unless you tell him. *Femme* and the Robin(s)' covers are as solid as the vault at Fort Knox."

"Still, the sooner I get you out of his sightline, the better I'll feel. The cake cutting is starting now, then Chloe will throw her bouquet and Josh the garter. After that, I'm pretty sure the newly married couple will leave. We can slip out right after them—that is, if you're up for some *extracurricular* activities at the hotel." He winked.

"Only if you brought your handcuffs." She returned the wink, adding a provocative smile.

Luke didn't miss a beat. "I never go anywhere with you without my handcuffs."

2

LUKE CAUGHT SIGHT of Rayla's parents as soon as he cleared the arrival gate and entered the McNamara Terminal at Detroit's Metropolitan Airport. He recognized them immediately because of pictures Rayla had shown him, as well as her precise descriptions. *Here we go. Meet the parents is on.*

He might have been more keyed into that usually fearful concept, except he was sidelined by Eliot and Camille Rousseau's striking physical attributes. They were youthful-looking and fit, and Rayla appeared to be a blend of both. If he'd had to choose between the two to say who Rayla resembled most, however, her father would win the toss. The shape, brilliance, and nuance of his eyes—like sapphires—matched those of his daughter's with uncanny precision. Yet, even more than the color he noted a familiar twinkle, a sparkle of mischief in those salient blue irises.

According to Rayla, her parents knew nothing of her or her grandmother's thieving vocations, yet an unmistakable strain of Rayla's roguish tenor seemed to nestle with equal intensity within her father's gaze as much as it did her own. If talking heredity, it was a small wonder. The Rousseau thieving legacy had begun with Eliot's grandfather, Pierre, and had been passed on to Pierre's sons, Adrien and Étienne. Evangeline Davis-Rousseau, Rayla's grandmother and the chief matriarch and founder of the Robin(s) of the Hood, had been the first and only thief on her side of the family.

As Rayla told it, *Grand-mère* Rousseau—or Gram, as she called her and Evie to everyone else—had met Étienne, the ten-year-older love of her life while vacationing on the Côte d'Azur at age sixteen. Falling completely in love, Evie had left her family a "see you later" note and took off with him. They'd not only married but had proceeded to become a thieving legend in southern France and most of Europe, though her family never knew about her illegal profession. Evie had returned to Michigan—Jackson, to be precise—to finish her high school education. During those two years, she'd lived with her new husband, and together, they'd trained Evie's best friend, Patti Nichol—later to become Patti Nichol-Sanders—in everything theft. Patti, already a superb artist, had easily developed a penchant for forgery, becoming one of the best art and ID forgers in the business. When the two ladies had graduated high school at age eighteen, they'd founded the Robin(s) of the Hood with Étienne's help and blessing.

Considering the Rousseau legacy, Luke found it hard to swallow Eliot had no knowledge of his grandfather's, uncle's, and parents' occupations while growing up in Paris and Nice. In fact, Luke was sure the man knew it all, and maybe Rayla's secret vocation, too.

Luke prided himself on his ability to read people. If he were any good at it, he'd deciphered all of Eliot's unspoken knowledge within minutes of his introduction to the man— specifically because of the way Dr. Eliot Rousseau sized him up. An upstanding, law-abiding federal agent dating his daughter should have elicited a pleasant response. Luke was seeing the exact opposite.

After Rayla hugged them, he extended his hand toward Camille and then Eliot, proffering the first greeting. "Hello, Drs. Rousseau. It's a pleasure to meet you."

Some of that impishness Luke had seen in Eliot's eyes loosened the man's tongue as soon as their hands connected. *"Bonjour, agent spécial Luke Keltry. Je comprends que vous parlez couramment ma langue maternelle, ainsi que de nombreuses autre langues?"*

Luke returned a smile. Taking virtually no time to translate the doctor's statement that he was aware Luke spoke his mother tongue and several other languages, he answered with an affirmative: *"Oui, Docteur Rousseau. Je fais en effet."*

"Quindi potremmo anche conversare in italiano, giusto?" Eliot pressed, switching to flawless Italian.

Luke nodded with appropriate appreciation to the man's questioning his ability to converse in that language, as well.

Then, *he* took control of Eliot's hunting expedition. Beginning in Italian, he informed the man he could accommodate him in that or any of the seven languages in which he was fluent and the six in which he was conversant, repeating his claim in each language. He was delighted to see his "turn of the tables" had impressed the reputable heart surgeon.

Rayla and her mother laughed. "My dad only speaks French, Italian, and a little Spanish, Luke," Rayla said.

"We've been learning Bengali," Camille interjected. "It's not required for our work in Bangladesh as there will be translators, but we took on the extra challenge."

Luke was impressed. The main reason Rayla had given him for the visit with her parents during this trip out east for Josh's wedding was because the Rousseau heart surgeons were leaving shortly for the impoverished areas of Bangladesh on a two-year medical mission with Doctors Without Borders. This would be her last opportunity to see her parents during that time span.

"I recognized your mention of Spanish, German, Russian, and Romanian," Eliot said. What were the others? In English." His lips twitched.

"Greek, Mandarin, Vietnamese, Korean, Farsi, and Hindi," Luke replied, noting the man's French-accented English.

A notably begrudging smile parted Eliot's tightly compressed lips. "Excellent. I would very much like to pick your brain in some of those languages. Unfortunate that Bengali isn't among them."

"Anyway, it's a pleasure to finally meet you, Luke," Camille said in flat, mid-western American English with a warmth that made him feel right at home. Wrapping an arm around Rayla, she addressed her daughter. "Let's get your bags and introduce Luke to your childhood home in Ann Arbor, shall we?"

Rayla kissed her mom on the cheek and hugged her again. "Sounds like a plan," she said.

After giving Luke the grand tour of the lavish Michigan home in which she grew up, Rayla swung them by the horseshoe kitchen bar where her mom had laid out a gourmet feast. Anything and everything anybody could possibly want to eat—Asian, Mexican, French, Italian, and all-American cuisine—stretched out in what looked to be perfect one-foot increments from one end of the countertop to the other. The food was prepared to perfection, too—just not by her mother. That was Mom. She spared no expense, but she'd never cooked a day in her life. Gram was the same way. *Without a doubt the reason I never learned to cook, either.*

Plates loaded down, she led Luke to the combination back porch/family room, where TV trays awaited. Sitting at a regular dining-room table was the other traditional custom her family rarely implemented. Trays in front of the TV had been the norm while she was growing up, and clearly, nothing had changed. Taking what had been her usual spot when she'd lived there with Luke sitting next to her, she noted the news footage running on the large flat-screen TV mounted on the far wall. Scooping up the remote, she raised the volume, her attention unwavering from the screen.

A jewel theft mentioned practically in passing. The commentators didn't have a clue about the ramifications of this particular heist. When the news anchorman moved on to the next story, Rayla returned the TV's volume to its original setting and tried to act normal. Her mother had noted her interest, however.

"I heard about that theft earlier today, before we left for the airport," Mom said. "It happened yesterday. I meant to mention it to you, honey. I know how much you love diamonds."

Rayla froze. The Levanger Lynx. A perfect diamond with a phenomenal link to two other diamonds. *And it was stolen on September 5th?* All the blood rushed from her head, and she felt like she might faint.

Her mother went on, oblivious to her swoon. "It was stolen from…"

Rayla tuned her out, filling in the blanks in her own head: *…from the Trondheim Museum of the Cultural Arts in Trondheim, Norway.* In and of themselves, neither the diamond nor the theft were of any notable consequence. She tried to calm herself. *Just because the Lynx has been successfully stolen, and on this specific date, doesn't mean the thief will go after the other two. But … What if he or she does?*

That would be of enormous consequence.

3

CONSIDERING HIS FBI EDUCATION, his snooping nature, and his natural ability for inductive and deductive reasoning, Luke knew three things before his stay with Rayla's parents was completed: One, Rayla's father knew all about his parents' thieving vocations but had opted for a different life. Two, Rayla didn't know her father was privy to the fact she had chosen the life he had rejected. And three, the doctor was worried as hell Luke was chasing Rayla as a thief, not as a girlfriend.

So, as soon as he said goodbye to Rayla at DTW to fly back to his pressing and relatively new job heading up the two-month-old west-coast High-End Theft Unit—leaving Rayla to spend a few more days with her parents—he called Evie Rousseau. Rayla's grandmother was as well-known to him as he was to her, every criminal aspect of her. As founder and first matriarch of the Robin(s) of the Hood, the final decision to welcome him as a friend of the thieving sisterhood had fallen to her, and he and Evie shared a mutual respect and positive relationship. So, having overheard the conversation Eliot had had with her in hushed, yet urgent French, behind the closed doors of the doctor's study—or at least what Eliot had thought were completely closed doors—Luke wanted a word with the woman. Not for himself or to get any help quelling Eliot's misgivings about him. Even Evie wouldn't have the ability to accomplish that. No, Luke wanted answers for Rayla.

"Hello, Luke," she answered his call with a pleasant tone. "Are you still in Michigan?"

"Hi, Evie. I'm at the airport in Detroit, waiting to fly back to LA. Rayla dropped me off. After having gotten through the screening process, I have about a forty-five-minute wait. I thought this would be a good time to call you. What is it, three-thirty in Paris?"

"*Oui,*" she answered with a laugh. "But it's not like you to call to chat. Something's on your mind, and I believe I know what it is."

He could have guessed as much. In so many ways, he and Evangeline Rousseau thought alike. The lady was a thief of the highest caliber and a force to be reckoned with, just like her granddaughter. Thing was, she had told him she felt he was an equal force. Quite the compliment, coming from her. Either that or her attempt to puff up his ego. He wanted to believe the former, but realism argued for the latter.

"You figured out the reason for Eliot's glaring," Evie pronounced.

"I did, but that's not why I'm calling. I know you talked to him, so I must believe you filled him in on our arrangement. I'm sure he's still suspicious of me, but, hopefully, time will take care of that. Besides, from what I can tell, Rayla's not that close to her parents, and she certainly won't be seeing them for at least another couple of years, at any rate."

"You're right," Evie replied. "I practically raised that girl. But, don't misunderstand. They all love each other immensely."

"I know."

"So, to what do I owe the pleasure, then?"

"I want to know why Rayla thinks her parents don't know about the Robin(s) and her *other* thieving vocation, because at least her father most certainly does."

"As you noted, her mother doesn't know, but Eliot has known what his father and I did for a living since he was a small child. We trained him to be a thief. When we gave him the option to follow in our path or choose his own, he chose a pre-med major at the University of Michigan. We gave him our blessing and let him go."

"But…"

"What about Rayla?" she filled in his pause. "He didn't want me to recruit her for the Robin(s), begged me not to. Technically, she wasn't in the direct line to join our sisterhood. The baton is passed on through daughters. Since I had no daughter, I initially passed my invitation to my sister Ava's daughter, Tarry. I had seen great promise in my niece at a very young age. I played little games with her to begin the training process whenever I saw her, but I waited much longer to ask her to join and then trained her when she'd accepted. I had no intention of telling my sister about my occupation or that I wanted to pursue her daughter for the sisterhood, so Tarry needed to be a legal adult. I recruited her on her eighteenth birthday. But what I saw in Rayla would have been a sin to postpone."

Luke snickered at the irony of her word choice.

"Never before have I witnessed such natural talent in a child," Evie continued. "So, I ignored my son's warnings to keep Rayla out of the sisterhood and went on to train her from the time she was seven."

"And Eliot just fell in and accepted it?"

Evie laughed, a soft, fond-remembrance kind of chuckle. "Not at first. Eliot was livid with me. He knew the moment he saw Rayla with the diamond necklace what I had done, but he also knew he couldn't do anything to reverse the decision. Rayla was excited to go through the training program, and Eliot knew she'd have the same option he'd had—to choose her own path when she'd completed the training and had become an adult. But besides that, my son couldn't deny the natural ability and superior talent his daughter possessed for everything theft. I think, deep down, he was, and still is, proud of her.

"Nevertheless, Camille has never known about Étienne and me, what we did for a living or the fact her husband could easily have been as good a thief as he is a heart surgeon. For obvious reasons, Eliot didn't want her to know any of it, especially that Rayla was now a part of that world, too. So, to make sure nothing slipped out accidentally, he decided I should tell Rayla that neither of them knew, and if she wanted to continue the course, become a bona fide member of the Robin(s) of the Hood, she could never tell either of them. I'd broken my son's first mandate by recruiting his daughter, but I went along with his second."

Luke questioned Evie's explanation. Rayla was as good an observer as she was a thief—*because* she was a thief. He'd seen the knowledge Eliot possessed in the man's glowering eyes, his concern for his daughter's freedom written all over his face. How did Rayla not see it? He posited the query to Evie.

"Eliot never looked at her the way he looked at you, Luke. He didn't have to. He's known all along what she is, what she's doing, and he's accepted it. He doesn't trust you because you're FBI. That's the only reason his reaction caught your attention. I'm sure Rayla noticed some odd looks from him here and there while she was growing up. Who's to know how she explained those away? But she most likely attributes the wariness Eliot exhibited toward you to him being a typical father sizing up a man with a dangerous career who has caught his daughter's eye in what could potentially be a long-term relationship."

That certainly made sense, enough to answer his question. But what was he supposed to do with the information? "So, now that I know the truth, I'm expected to keep it from her? I wasn't in on the original deal between you and your son. I don't feel obligated to uphold it."

Another soft chuckle preceded Evie's response. "Good. You knew pretty much all of what I told you before you called me. If you don't bring me into it and don't tell Rayla that you confirmed it with me beforehand, I'd be grateful for you to broach the subject with her. As far as I'm concerned, it's high time she knew. If it were up to me, I'd tell Camille, too."

"You want me to just up and tell her I think her father knows she's a thief, knows you're a thief, and that he could have been one, too? I can't imagine how she'd react to that."

"As I said, if you leave out the part about confirming with me, Rayla will do what she does so well: follow the evidence and find the truth. Then, it will be up to her whether or not to confront her father."

"Following the evidence will lead her to you first. Are you ready to tell her you've been keeping this from her? That while training her as a thief, you failed to mention her father had undergone the same instruction so many years before? Geez, Evie, I've got to believe that's going to rock her world a little."

"Right down to its very core, no doubt, but it's the only way now. You are who you are—a federal agent whose suspicions led him to dig up some dirt. Since the dirt is within your girlfriend's family, there's no way an honorable man such as yourself can keep it from her. You came by the suspicion naturally, so in the same natural way you'll share it with her. Decades of deceit will be uncovered, and all because you are very good at what you do, Special Agent Luke Keltry. And, I, for one, am very glad for it."

It was everything he could do not to roll his eyes. "Right." With a significant sigh, he said, "One other question while I have your undivided attention?"

"Certainly."

"What's the special significance of the jewel theft which occurred in Norway on Saturday? Rayla was suspiciously distracted by it, and not in a good way."

4

As soon as she dropped Luke off at flight departures, Rayla breezed onto I-94 West for the thirty-minute drive back to Ann Arbor. She was meeting her parents for lunch at noon downtown, which gave her plenty of time to return to her childhood home, but what with it being such a beautiful, early-autumn day and her having a couple hours to kill, she chose instead to visit her favorite spot on the U of M campus—Nichols Arboretum. There, she found a suitable bench overlooking the Huron River to make her call to Gram.

She couldn't deny the alarm which had consumed her upon hearing of the heist in Norway. She'd wanted to call her grandmother immediately, but she knew that wouldn't have been her wisest move. Luke was fed-trained to the bone. She wouldn't have been able to sneak out without him hearing her, and he easily could have followed and listened in. The details surrounding this heist weren't anything she wanted him to know about ... at least not yet. So, she waited out the rest of Sunday, all day Monday, and breakfast this morning—with considerable impatience—until she could obtain the privacy needed to hash through it with Gram, and maybe all the Robin(s). With great anticipation, she tapped her grandmother's picture in her iPhone's Favorites.

Unfortunately, the call went straight to voicemail. *Gram has her phone turned off? Why?* She had never known the woman to turn off her phone. The Robin(s)' leader was on call twenty-four-seven, and she never wanted to miss calls from anyone else, either, even though the six-hour time difference with Michigan and nine-hour difference with California sometimes became a factor. *But it's only three-forty in Paris. What's going on?* Even if Gram had an appointment, she'd silence the ringer, not turn off the phone. Sure, she probably wouldn't hear or answer the call, but it would ring several times before going to voicemail. This time, though, it hadn't rung at all.

With another moment's musing, Rayla calmed herself. *She's probably on another call.* A second later, Gram's text came in confirming that theory, and she breathed a sigh of relief. Her grandmother would return her call as soon as she could. Tightly clutching the phone, Rayla waited for that callback while her mind raced through everything she knew about this particular heist and the possibility, maybe likelihood, for the other thefts.

Some fifty years or so prior, someone had done his homework. Probably some second-story man, laid up and recovering from a fall, or worse, during a job gone wrong with too much time on his hands. Gram hadn't given specific details about who had put together the facts on this heisting-lore and had started the challenge, stating only that it was for real and all the information was factual—starting with The Levanger Lynx.

The Lynx was originally found on Monday, September 5, 1887, lying on top of the soil near the mid-western banks of the Trondheim Fjord in Levanger, Norway by a copper mining excavator. Aksel Helberg recognized his find as a rough diamond, and soon had an expert appraisal. Once cut and polished, the one-hundred-five carat, Ideal-cut, perfectly flawless and colorless Marquise-shape Brilliant was sold to an internationally renowned diamond aficionado, eventually coming to rest on display at Trondheim Museum of the Cultural Arts. In itself a fabulous find and a worthy diamond to possess—with an estimated value of roughly $100M U.S. dollars in the current market—it was, at some point, discovered to be the first find of three incredible, cross-culturally-linked diamonds.

Rayla looked off dreamily, remembering the first time she'd seen The Lynx in its display when Gram had taken her on a tour of Europe's finest diamonds. That was when she learned the remarkable story of the "Triple Crown," the age-old heisting challenge some thief had penned, and also when Gram had sternly cautioned her never to steal any of the diamonds from that challenge—not individually or for the challenge. These were not diamonds reputable thieves stole. Period.

The second diamond of the mysteriously-linked trio, The Contessa of Kimberley, was mined from the Kimberley, South Africa mine one week after the first—on Monday, September 12, 1887. Cut and polished to be an Ideal-cut Cushion-shape, the one-hundred-twelve carat, perfectly flawless and colorless gem sailed through the ranks of ownership via the most popular names in diamond mining, beginning with De Beers. Eventually, The Contessa was purchased by a particularly good-hearted philanthropist and put on display at The Cape Town Diamond Museum in South Africa. Rayla had only seen pictures of that magnificent gem, which was valued at $125M USD in today's market.

The third diamond, the one she was most familiar with and for which she carried great concern now, was discovered on the banks of St. Marys River in Sault Ste. Marie, Michigan, on Monday, September 19, 1887—exactly one week after The Contessa's discovery and two weeks after The Levanger Lynx—during the rebuilding of the old Fort Brady into the New Fort Brady in Michigan's Upper Peninsula. The Maiden of St. Marys, as it was soon named, was found a few inches below the soil by Army Corporal John Pinchot. The stone was to become a one-hundred-nineteen carat Ideal-cut Brilliant Oval. Perfectly flawless and colorless just like the other two, The Maiden was a multi-faceted sparkler the size of a small egg. Corporal Pinchot put the diamond on display in the newly constructed, two-month-old Grand Hotel on Mackinac Island, Michigan, where it has resided in different, updated displays to this day.

Since 1987, the entirety of her life and then some, the resplendent gem had remained affixed within a "theft-proof" casing in the center portion of a tastefully elegant chandelier. The five-foot-long crystal and diamond light source could be viewed dangling through an opening in the middle of Grand's fifth and sixth floors—the Cupola Bar at the very center and top of the hotel. The diamond display/chandelier extended downward from the upper portion of the hotel's highest point, the cupola—a tower, or "widow's watch"—through a central opening, providing the connection for the two-floor Cupola Bar. The extravagant area of both floors afforded not only the viewing of The Maiden of St. Marys, but also a breathtaking, one-hundred-eighty-degree panorama of the Straights of Mackinac—the area where Lake Huron and Lake Michigan came together—and the Mackinac Bridge. At five miles in length, the "Mighty Mac" had connected Michigan's Lower Peninsula to its Upper Peninsula since 1957 and remained to this day the longest suspension bridge between two anchorages in the Western Hemisphere.

Rayla knew all of it well. Her parents had taken her to the Mackinac area, and specifically to the Island, at the end of every summer as soon as she returned from Gram's in France and right before school started up. They always stayed at Grand Hotel on the island for the duration of their vacation, usually a week to ten days. And it was indeed grand. The hotel was kept in the fashion of the 19th Century, and therefore unique, but then so was the entire island which housed it. To her knowledge, nothing like Mackinac Island existed anywhere in the world for one delightful reason: Motor vehicles were prohibited. The entire island operated with horses, buggies, and bicycles.

The Maiden of St. Marys, hanging dutifully and brilliantly in Grand's Cupola Bar chandelier, had always been a special diamond to her. The thought of some thug or thugs stealing it caused bile to rise in her throat. That stupid heisting challenge had gone unclaimed for at least half a century. Why would anyone suddenly decide to take up that gauntlet now? The best thieves, the only ones capable of successfully perpetrating these heists, were high-end, and most high-end thieves had *some* moral code. They wouldn't touch it. Of course, there were unprincipled high-end thieves out there. Rayla had just never met any.

Sure, each diamond was worth $100M or more—The Maiden itself the most valuable, estimated at $150M. And there was, of course, the "hinging on the magically bizarre" coupling of the three stones. First, one had to consider the fact the trio of diamonds had been discovered exactly one week apart, in succession, in the same month and year—September, 1887. Second, the fact each diamond uncannily had been cut to somewhat match with the date it had been discovered: The Levanger Lynx, discovered on September 5th having a final carat weight of one-hundred-five; The Contessa of Kimberley, discovered on September 12th with a one-hundred-twelve carat weight; and The Maiden of St. Marys, discovered on September 19th with a one-hundred-nineteen carat weight.

But really, someone taking up a challenge to steal all three and providing proof each gem had been lifted on the specific day it had been found—three thefts perpetrated exactly one week apart? To what end? Merely to have accomplished it? The diamonds certainly couldn't be fenced for more than a third of their value, if that; they were too well-known. Hardly seemed worthwhile, except for the glory. *Or, maybe to display on the glory-seeker's mantle?*

According to Gram, when the challenge had been introduced into the thieving community, it had been set up to mirror The Triple Crown in horse racing. Each race of the well-known grand trio was always run in the same order and at

23

the same spaced time intervals every year—Kentucky Derby, first Saturday in May; Preakness, third Saturday in May; and Belmont Stakes, third Saturday following the Preakness. Thus, this heisting challenge carried the moniker, "The Triple Crown." Catchy, but who was around now to care if the challenge were completed? None of it made any sense.

Her phone buzzing then sounding its familiar tune in her hand startled her. *Gram.* Maybe she'd get some answers now.

5

LUKE LANDED AT LAX, met up with his FBI escort, and arrived at the FBI LA field office at around one p.m. Pacific Time. He was still operating on Eastern Time, making it four o'clock for him, which was perfectly doable, but being *summoned* to stop off here by his new boss, the new Assistant Special Agent in Charge of LA's Major Thefts, ruffled his feathers. Since this new guy wanted to meet immediately upon his arrival back in California, Luke had had to land in LA, at the city's crazy-busy airport. He and Rayla had flown out of Santa Barbara, where he'd left his Chevy Colorado in long-term parking. Thus, he had no vehicle of his own in LA.

The new ASAC was most accommodating in getting him from the airport to the LA Bureau by sending the agent escort, but Luke was sure he'd have to rent something for the two-hour drive to his and Rayla's condo in Montecito when this completely unnecessary, "Hi. Nice to meet you," rendezvous was over. *Probably won't take five minutes ... if that.* Not his idea of a great use of his time or money.

When he'd taken the new west-coast HETU position, he hadn't been too sure how he'd get along with ASAC Phil Brooke, the head of LA's Major Thefts Department upon Luke's arrival, especially after the exceptional relationship he'd had with his previous boss in DC. Supervisory Special Agent Dave Knapp, founder and leader of the first High-End Theft Unit, would be a hard act to follow for anyone, but with Brooke gone, this new guy was stacking up to be a serious step in the wrong direction. *Certainly not earning any brownie points with me.*

The guy didn't even tell him his name. All Luke got was a text on Saturday from "New ASAC of LA's Major Thefts," instructing him to get his ass into the LA field office ASAP on Tuesday—today—when he returned to California. When Luke texted back that he wasn't flying into LA, the ASAC told him—more precisely, ordered him—to change his flight plans. The SOB had only been there one day and already he'd proven to have a superiority complex that screamed "major pain in the ass."

Using every iota of his parents' superior upbringing and his FBI training to adjust his facial expression to something more pleasant before meeting this asshole, Luke stepped off the elevator and traversed the fourth-floor hallways to Major Thefts. Ready to knock, he saw the door was slightly ajar. He knocked anyway. No way he wanted to get off on the wrong foot with a man who could surely make his life a living hell on a daily basis.

But his mouth fell open when he saw the man who greeted him at the door.

"You look pretty calm, Luke. I'm impressed. After all the bullshit I fed you, I half expected you to come in here with steam shooting out of your ears." The new ASAC then proceeded to push Luke's hanging jaw shut.

He finally found his voice. "Dave Knapp... You son of a bitch!" He clasped his old, and now once again current, boss's arm and allowed the man to pull him into a brief man-hug. "What the hell, Dave? You going to follow me wherever I go?"

"Somebody's got to keep you in line." Dave pushed a stack of boxes aside and waved Luke through the department bullpen and into his private office.

"This must've just happened over the weekend," Luke said when seated on the one vacant chair. "When I flew out last Thursday evening, I had no idea Brooke was leaving Major

Thefts. I tried to call you when I landed in Virginia. I hoped to scrape together enough time to see you and maybe the rest of the team for lunch or something, but my call kept going to voicemail. I finally called Cheryl. She said you were out of town. I take it you told her not to tell me?"

"Surprise!" Dave snickered as he sat on the corner of his desk. "I didn't know you were flying to Virginia until Cheryl told me you called her. Timing sure wasn't the greatest, but yeah, LA's Drugs, Gangs, and Major Thefts ASAC Valerie Palmieri called me Thursday morning. Phil Brooke left in a hurry. He was already gone when I flew out that evening. I met with her on Friday, and she offered me the promotion on the spot. Cheryl and the kids were excited about moving to LA, so here I am. My lovely and awesome wife is taking care of listing the house and packing up. Meanwhile, I thought you'd like to know, I'm not, in fact, setting up here; I'm cleaning out Brooke's office. Major Thefts has relocated to the Ventura satellite office. Since your new HETU is the only unit under Major Thefts, ADIC Kingston thought we were the best department to move in next to HETU in that new space the LA Bureau accrued and renovated next to the Ventura office."

Luke's brain filled in the unspoken significance of Kingston's title. *Assistant Director in Charge Bernard Kingston— head honcho of the LA FBI field office.*

Dave continued, "I met my team of agents yesterday, and they pretty much had everything in here ready to move. I sent them to Ventura behind the moving van to get set up. There were a few items from Brooke's office I had to deal with, which I completed today. After arranging for another pickup for these boxes, my next project is to find a place to rent in or near Ventura until Cheryl and I can look around properly for a house. That's the primary reason I wanted you to stop off here on your way home. I thought we could ride over to your neck of the woods together, have some dinner, and maybe you could lend a hand with that?"

Luke heard and understood the strain in Dave's voice. He knew firsthand how stressful changing jobs and moving across country could be. The last two months, spent transferring himself and all his belongings to California and assembling his team at the FBI Ventura satellite office, had been chaotic.

He'd finished interviewing candidates and hired his four-man, one-woman HETU team—six agents in all, including him—within two weeks, but getting everyone settled in their new digs had been time-consuming. Thankfully, he hadn't needed to add "looking for a place to live" to his agenda as did Dave, but he had other Bureau-inflicted grief to deal with. Specifically, what Dave had referred to earlier: that "new space" at the Ventura location.

The FBI had bought out the leases of the two companies that shared the building with the satellite office, making the entire one-story, beige stucco structure completely Bureau owned. The purchase allotted the LA Bureau and Ventura office some needed space—twenty-five-hundred square feet of extra space to be exact. But, before anybody moved in, the building was remodeled to bring it up to FBI standards and to divide the space according to need. Luke had learned early in the remodeling process that he and his tiny HETU team would get the short end of the stick, but he wasn't complaining. A thousand or so of those square feet—with a private office for him and a suitably-sized bullpen for the other five members—belonged to the High-End Theft Unit at the far east end. Plenty of space and only slightly smaller than DC's HETU office. Since neither Major Thefts nor HETU were affiliated with the Ventura satellite office, but rather were extensions of the LA field office, their areas were left separated by the nice thick wall already in place.

Until the upgrades were accomplished, Luke had sequestered the far southeast corner of the satellite office's space, not even marginally far enough away to be separated from them. Thankfully, the head of that office, Supervisory

Senior Resident Agent Jennifer Woodward, let him use the visiting guest office to conduct his HETU candidate interviews—the same office he'd occupied when he'd been assigned to help with the apprehension of the Pacific Coast robbers. The remodeling project took a mere month, another plus, allowing Luke to get himself and his team moved into HETU's new office space before he left for Josh's wedding.

Besides his new job as Supervisory Special Agent of the west coast HETU and Dave's new job as ASAC of LA's Major Thefts, SSRA Jen Woodward had taken another position within the Bureau hierarchy and left the Ventura office. Luke had met the new agent in charge briefly before taking off with Rayla for DC. SSRA Barbara Sutherlin and her second in command, Assistant Resident Agent, ARA, Debra Sines, who'd worked together previously in LA, showed up last Thursday, minutes before Luke left. With complete chaos in the Ventura office and HETU's move next door, for sure it was not the ideal time to take a vacation, short though it was.

He lobbed Dave a smile. "You have Bureau-issued transportation at this point?"

"I do."

"In that case, I'd be glad to show you around." Luke glanced at his watch. "Have you seen the Ventura office yet?"

"No. I was hoping you'd be okay with stopping there first."

"I need to check in with my team, too. It's about an hour drive if traffic's flowing well. We should be there by three if we leave now."

Dave gathered his things. Handing Luke two boxes and picking up a couple more, he laid a hand on his shoulder. "I dub you my west-coast tour guide. Let's go."

6

EXASPERATING. Y*ES,* THAT WAS IT. That was how she'd describe her grandmother. Maybe not all the time, but Gram certainly could be one of the most infuriating individuals on the planet—at least in Rayla's world. And the woman had done her due diligence to maintain that trait with her during their last phone conversation.

We're to do nothing? Just wait and see if the next diamond is stolen before talking through any plan to stop the final theft? No way could she go along with her grandmother on this one. The Contessa of Kimberley needed protection, at the very least a good thief following the despicable one if the gem were stolen. But, of course, Gram was way ahead of any plan Rayla might have entertained to accomplish that feat.

"The Robin(s) have need of your services right there in the Midwest, honey," Gram had said. Then she went on to lay out another loathsome theft ring which the cagey lady knew would capture her attention with at least as much if not significantly more intrigue as the possibility of the perpetration of the second leg in The Triple Crown theft.

Corvettes. Lots of them. And Gram knew Rayla had a soft spot for Vettes.

Some odious group being touted as high-end thieves by the press were stealing the sleek American sports cars from reputable dealers throughout the Midwest and selling them on the black market. Rayla was wise enough to know Gram put her on this case solo with the hope it would keep her occupied

31

through the time The Contessa was supposed to be stolen, according to the challenge. But she had every intention of wrapping up the Vette job with plenty of time to set herself up in Cape Town where The Contessa was displayed.

Gram hadn't counted on the help the five other youngest Robin(s) were willing to give Rayla, despite the "busy work" she had heaped on them specifically to render them incapable of assisting her "headstrong granddaughter." Gram had grossly underestimated the mad computer capabilities and the bond among the six. Now that they were all working together out of the Santa Barbara ARI office, they'd become closer than ever. One might even say, "thick as thieves."

A call-to-action text to the five in Santa Barbara was all it took. Her best friend, Devon Hunter, her three second cousins, Tami, Wendy, and Laura Martin—the daughters of her first cousin, once removed, who Rayla had always called "Aunt Tarry"—and her good friend and last of the third generation Robin(s) of the Hood, Krista Caine, hopped on the first flight out of Santa Barbara and met up with her at Detroit Metro at about the same time Luke had found out his old boss from DC HETU was now once again his boss as ASAC of Major Thefts.

Rayla had talked to Luke while waiting for her cohorts to arrive at the gate and depart their plane, telling him she'd be held up a little longer in the Midwest because of a Robin(s) job Gram had given her. Her FBI honey knew better than to ask about the job. That was part of the pact he'd made when he'd met the members of the sisterhood and was granted the right to be one of the few outsiders, and the only fed … or anyone in law enforcement … to have access to them and to continue his relationship with Rayla. The Robin(s) agreed to help him solve cases for which he could use their assistance, and vice versa, and he'd agreed to let them operate as they always had without questions or interference. Since she'd told him this was a Robin(s) case, Rayla knew he wouldn't ask.

What she intended to do for The Contessa was a different story, but Luke didn't know anything about that.

Her generally law-abiding beau had negotiated specific limitations for her as *Thief à la Femme*, restrictions he controlled—or thought he did. In fact, he was under the impression he made all the decisions about what she could steal as *Thief à la Femme*. Silly man. The renegade spirit that soared within her couldn't possibly buckle under any restraint, even the arguably reasonable ones Luke had imposed. The words "imposed" and "restraint" were key. *Thief à la Femme*/Rayla Rousseau would not have anything imposed upon her, nor could she be restrained … unless, of course, it was her idea.

Her face and neck warmed at the thought of that *other* meaning for restraint between her and Luke. *Mmm. Those handcuffs.* Never mind he'd put her in them for non-playful incidents, as well. She smiled again at the double meaning Luke had imparted when he'd said he never went anywhere with her without them. The iron bracelets couldn't hold her captive in any case—except when she desired.

Lightheadedness and a familiar buzz of pleasure elicited a warmth throughout her body as she continued to dwell on Luke and his special techniques of enticement. She missed him so much already, and he'd only been gone a little over six hours. Devon calling her name cajoled her back to reality.

Six bubbling women, hugging, smiling, and all talking at once spread their contagious joy throughout the baggage claim area, causing people all around them to smile, as well. Once the youngest generation Robin(s)' bags were claimed, Rayla led the way to the SUV she'd rented for her extended stay in Michigan. There, they piled in and continued jabbering as if they hadn't seen one another in months rather than the three days it had been. *Lord, I love these women!*

Rayla hustled them into Ann Arbor for dinner at a casual, college-town restaurant and bar. Tucked away in a corner booth, and in very hushed tones, Devon brought her up to date on all intel she and the others had gathered before boarding their flight to Michigan. As usual, the five had done a remarkable job of collecting the necessary data, both from the FBI and the dark web, to defeat this reprehensible Vette threat.

Put simply, they had been able to pinpoint the next burglary right down to the date and time the theft would be perpetrated. One third-generation Robin(s) thief was a hacking force to be contended with. Five of them all on the same information-gathering mission were comparable to super-heroes.

But with all intel from their numerous sources laid out, Rayla was bummed with the accumulated evidence. This was a crew of thieves using an inside-man at the various dealerships that had already been robbed, and that was what they planned for the last burglary scheduled for the upcoming weekend. The best way to catch all of them was to stake out the area, allow the theft to occur, follow the thieves to their stash, and then call in the local LEOs to apprehend the culprits with their vehicular booty. No problem, except, according to the dark-web chat rooms heralding the thieves, the theft was scheduled for early Saturday morning, sometime after midnight. There was no way she'd make it to South Africa to save The Contessa.

"I'm glad you guys came, but you all knew before you flew out this is at most a two-man job. Why did you all come?"

Krista laughed. "Evie's 'busy-work' took us all of five minutes. We were bored. It was like a sign from heaven when you called."

Rayla added a grin to her nod. "I guess we can double up and surround the place. That'll make the bust that much easier. Unfortunately, it won't help me with The Contessa at all." With a heavy sigh, she tried to clear her mind and set it to the task at hand, but before she uttered another word, Devon cut her off.

"We've got this, Rayla. We'll take these guys down without you. Promise. Go save The Contessa."

She thought about that for a minute. This Vette threat was exactly the type of job she would have paid to get involved in. Her love for Corvettes made this the perfect Robin(s) or *Thief à la Femme* caper for her. How could she walk away from this one, a definite and legitimate threat, to pursue protecting a diamond on another continent from a *possible* theft for which there was no chatter at all online? *I can't, and Gram knows it.*

Maybe Gram was right. Maybe The Contessa hadn't been targeted. After all, there was no mention of this crazy challenge being underway through any of their vast Internet sources. And, even if The Contessa was targeted, there was nothing to say the thief or thieves could pull off the second heist. She cocked her head with a sly smile. *Especially if the local LEOs in Cape Town are given an anonymous heads-up.* Satisfied she'd thought it through and made the right decision, she informed the others.

"Are you sure, Ray?" Tami asked. "You know we'll gladly handle this if you want to go to Cape Town."

The other four Robin(s) chimed in their agreement.

"I'm sure. I can't sit still all night for a *possible* theft when there are Corvettes … *Vettes*, for cryin' out loud … being stolen and hacked up right here under my nose. I need to be with you. Gram knew what she was doing when she told me about this job." Her intended grunt turned into more of a giggle. "That's why my astute grandmother is the head and we merely make up the tail of our righteous-thieving snake."

She took another few seconds to laugh that out before continuing. "All right. We have actionable intel on the final theft scheduled for the upcoming weekend at the GM Bowling Green Assembly in Bowling Green, Kentucky. As you all know, that location is dedicated to rolling out Vettes and is the only plant in the world that builds the American sports car." She paused and panned the group. They had all worked well with one another on countless occasions, so it made no difference to her how they handled her next question. "Anyone have a preference for who you'd like to team up with to surround that facility?"

When no one spoke up, Wendy summed up the ladies' sentiments. "It doesn't matter to us, Ray, but I think we all agree, with your love for Vettes, you should definitely be the one to head up this operation and decide on the best way to nail these guys."

7

"You're asking questions I believe I've already answered."
Luke kept his voice even and his tone light, his eyes fixed
straight ahead as Dave drove them down U.S. 101. But inside,
he was sorely losing patience with his friend and boss. The man
hadn't stopped grilling him about his former obsession since
Rayla had called and the ride to Ventura had begun. "I told you,
I haven't had any time to pursue either *Thief à la Femme* or any
of the Robin(s) since I was assigned to the Pacific-Coast
burglary-turned-armed-robbery case. As soon as that was
completed, I got the job offer out here, and my life has been
nothing but utter madness since. Besides, another female
captivates my thoughts these days."

"Interesting that *Thief à la Femme* entangled herself in the
Pacific-coast case, ultimately finding most of the stolen goods
and returning them to the very FBI office you were working
out of. A bit too much of a coincidence, I'd say, especially since
I don't believe in coincidences."

He squelched a desire to suggest that, just maybe, *Thief à
la Femme* was as enamored with him as he had been with her.
Not a good idea to continue linking the two of us either way.
"Whether you believe in them or not, sometimes they happen,"
he replied instead, hoping his inner grin wasn't visible on his
face. Dave had been right. It was no coincidence.

"Even if that's true, you managed to snag yourself a
girlfriend I'm told is remarkably similar to the young lady you
identified as the Robin(s) thief who fought with you in

Arlington. A single coincidence is one thing, but two? I don't think so. It's her, isn't it, Luke?"

"How do you know what my girlfriend looks like?"

"I looked up your friend from White Collar, and we've had a conversation or two."

Josh would never give up the under-the-table assistance he supplied, helping me find Rayla when she used the Nicole Renault alias. For sure, Dave must have kept those conversations light, appearing to be interested in what Luke had been up to since moving to California. Josh told Dave about Rayla with no reason to believe she was anything but what Luke had told him. His buddy hadn't shown the least bit of suspicion about Rayla until he met her the day before his wedding. Luke was sure Josh hadn't talked to Dave since then, but now both were skeptical of Rayla, entertaining the possibility she could be one if not both thieves Luke had obsessed over. *This has to stop. Right here. Right now.*

"Rayla's not the thief I tangled with. Trust me, I'd know. Of course she's similar. Shit, she looks like she could be her twin. Long dark hair, big blue eyes, figure that would stop a freight train. That's my type, Dave. I met her while staying at the Hilton Santa Barbara Beachfront Resort. We were on a couple of surfboards, riding out a particularly invigorating wave, and ran into each other—literally. I was vacationing specifically to mourn having lost my Jane Doe Robin(s)' trail. Rayla was staying at the resort while looking for a place to rent or buy for her new job at American Riviera Innovations. We went for drinks, then dinner, and, well ... I'm sure you must remember something about how the dating thing goes—ancient history that it is for you notwithstanding." He broke off to smirk at Dave, who showed his appreciation by flipping him off.

"So, when I was reassigned here and she asked me to move in with her, I didn't bat one eyelash," Luke continued, unabated. "It's been heaven ever since." His and Rayla's story was absolutely nothing near what he'd just imparted, but Dave wouldn't have a clue he'd lied. Luke was sure. His thieving, con-artist girlfriend had come up with that story when it became clear she'd be thrust into situations with the FBI—parties, gatherings, and such—where he'd introduce her as his girlfriend. Not to mention chats with Josh and her meeting him for the wedding. Although he considered himself pretty good at the deceit thing, the irrepressible *Thief à la Femme* had given him valuable lessons in the fine art of lying—much more believably. *And I mastered it brilliantly, if I do say so myself.*

"I'm sure it has been," Dave replied to Luke's heaven statement with an upward flick of his head. "Rayla Rousseau, huh?" he pressed. "There's not much information on her anywhere online. No Facebook, Instagram, Twitter, or Snapchat accounts. In fact, she's not on any social media at all, nor is there much background info on her. Doesn't that strike you as odd?"

Luke sighed, faced his boss, and dove into the rehearsed spiel he and Rayla had prepared. "It did, until I asked her about it, and she had a perfectly good explanation—one her parents backed up when I met them. The doctors Rousseau are world-renowned heart surgeons and extremely wealthy. They kept all information about Rayla, including her birth and any and all records of her off-grid, hoping to ward off the possibility of kidnapping for ransom. Apparently, it's a common practice among wealthy doctors at U of M." He put up a hand, effectively halting Dave's next question. "Once she was an adult and on her own, she decided she didn't want or need social media in her life. She's never been the type to walk around with a cellphone glued in front of her eyes. She hates that. Rayla's every bit the sports slash outdoor activities oriented girl. She'd rather surf, sky dive, or do anything sports-related, especially run, than just about anything else."

"Qualified for the last Olympic Marathon trials, I understand," Dave said. "Seems like that would have gotten her some press. Yet, I can't find her name listed as a participant."

Luke kept his temper in check. Dave would question everything about Rayla now that he'd talked to Josh and poked around online. It was his nature, and also why he was such a good FBI agent. Luke needed to ride it out, let Dave get his answers as needed. Any show of irritation on his part would further raise his boss's suspicions.

"She didn't compete in the trials. She couldn't. She was in France working out an internship for her Electronics Engineering major. Since she declined the honor as soon as she found out, the next lady in line was the one listed in the news release." He glanced at Dave. "How'd you know about that, anyway?" Luke rolled his eyes. "Never mind. Clearly, you've been using your FBI clout to dig into her background thoroughly on my behalf. Not that it's necessary. I'm FBI, too, remember? You don't think I executed my own check on her?"

"I hoped you had, but I've noted you can be temporarily blinded by females that fit your *Thief à la Femme* and that specific Robin(s)' profile."

That much was true.

"Still got that bruise on your shin?"

His grunt mutated to a chuckle. "That tango happened four months ago. What do you think?" If he rolled his eyes anymore, Luke was sure he'd become permanently dizzy. "Okay. You made your point. Check her out all you like. I can't believe you'll find any more dirt on her than I did, but if it makes you happy, have at it."

"What kind of dirt?"

Luke let loose a laugh and allowed his roguish side to take main stage. "Brace yourself." He leaned over and whispered, "Her father is *really* French—you know, a *real typical Frenchie*, born and raised in Paris and Nice. And get this. He got her mother pregnant with Rayla while they were in college together—sophomore year. Luckily, they really were in love, so they got married and had their one and only baby girl when they were both twenty years old. Since Rayla's paternal grandparents picked up the responsibility to see to Rayla's needs, both Eliot and Camille were able to continue their undergraduate college educations and go on to med school at the University of Michigan. Pretty racy stuff, huh?" *And all true, too.*

Dave was now the one to roll his eyes. Unfortunately, he recovered quickly.

"What about your Interpol buddy? What was his name? He must be texting you on a regular basis, keeping you up to date with *Thief à la Femme* and the Robin(s)' whereabouts. Are the thieving ladies still around here, targeting the west coast? We haven't seen or heard anything about them in the DC HETU since you left."

"You're talking about Ed, Edgar Bristol, out of the Interpol London office, but he and I only tracked *Femme* together. He doesn't have any interest in the Robin(s). He's texted me a few times, telling me our girl has been busy on the European circuit. Quite busy, according to him." Lies. All lies. Luke's last correspondence with Ed about a week ago entailed Ed asking if he knew what had happened to *Femme*. Boy, did he, but Ed didn't get any of his exclusive intel, nor would Dave.

Dave's probing questions aside, the biggest problem Luke had encountered when he took the job here on the west coast was the condo situation. Josh had investigated who was renting Rayla's condo because Luke had asked him to, off-book and very under-the-table. As such, Josh knew Nicole Renault, Rayla's alias which he'd found via his FBI search on that property, was the Robin(s) thief Luke had been chasing.

Having asked Josh to get involved came back to bite him when he and Rayla had worked out their differences and started a relationship. She didn't want to move out of her condo, but with Josh in the loop on Luke's pursuit of her as one of the

Robin(s) of the Hood, she couldn't stay under the Nicole Renault alias. So, the two of them put their heads together and worked out the perfect solution. "Nicole" moved out, and Rayla *bought* the condo under her real name.

They had prepared an "everyone's got a doppelganger" story, but it never came up. Ocean Crest Condominiums had been sold to another company, and Rayla's hair had grown out considerably from the haircut and funky dye job she'd implemented to evade him, enough to snip out most of the purple stripe. She used her authentic Rayla Lynn Rousseau driver's license for the condo purchase. Nobody at the closing knew anything about Nicole Renault because Rayla had *rented* the condo under that alias. Worked out perfectly, especially when Luke told Josh he'd turned Rayla onto the vacated condo when "Nicole" once again fled from him. The fact Rayla's parents were wealthy enough to pay for it in cash sold the story even more, though Rayla had been the one to pay for it.

Seeing the exit for Ventura, Luke was more than happy to have a reason to quell Dave's interrogation. "Here we are. I hope you've been paying attention. This is exit number 64 off U.S. 101—South Victoria Ave. Take it."

8

AT THE END OF THE EXIT RAMP, Luke instructed Dave to turn left, and they followed South Victoria, which curved back and ran parallel with 101, for a couple miles. Another left onto Knoll Drive and a quarter mile or so got them to the FBI Ventura office.

Dave pulled into the parking space assigned to him, the one with his title practically glowing in bright yellow paint: ASAC Major Thefts. With a snicker in his tone, he said, "I now have another valuable piece of information from my journey out west. Besides learning how to navigate LAX, I can get from the LA FBI field office to the Ventura satellite office."

"Baby steps, boss. It's a big state."

"And my very own private parking space? This is too good to be true!" His head snapped to Luke, who spoke up before he asked.

"No, I do not have my own private parking space. I'm sure that'll make you feel all the more important and appreciated."

Outside the car with boxes in hand, they veered to the right side of the elongated, one story building—the newly renovated LA field office annex. The Ventura satellite office occupied the left portion of the structure, and the two maintained separate entrances. Major Thefts and HETU shared an entrance, but the two departments were housed in separate rooms connected by an entryway and door which could be locked.

Inside, Dave's agents clamored to help with the boxes. When everyone was settled, Luke called in his crew from the back office and introduced them to Dave. Dave reciprocated, rattling off the names of the nine special agents who made up LA's Major Thefts. Luke was impressed Dave remembered his new team members' names, given he'd been introduced to them only the day before, but the introductions had been unnecessary. Luke had worked with all the agents in Major Thefts when he'd first arrived in LA back in June. As expected, Dave's agents and Luke's HETU team had greeted each other upon Major Thefts' arrival at the Ventura office. Both teams seemed to be getting along nicely.

After Luke spent close to an hour dealing with overdue paperwork, Dave trekked through the unlocked and open doorway between their departments and knocked on Luke's office door, which Luke had left open.

"I'm ready to go whenever you are," he said,

"Now works for me," Luke replied.

As they cleared the outer building doorway, Luke suggested they stop into the Ventura satellite office. "I think it'd be good for interoffice relations to prove we're not a couple snobbish, arrogant east-coast SOBs, by taking the initiative to introduce ourselves. Besides, they have a new SSRA and ARA over there, too. I didn't get more than a handshake and a 'nice to meet you' in before I took off in a hurry to catch my plane last Thursday evening. I'd like to make sure I didn't piss anyone off."

Dave lobbed a smile that traveled through his eyes and into his hairline. "Luke Keltry piss someone off? I don't think that's possible. Even if you did, all you'd have to do is apologize." He eyed Luke, inquisitively. "Women or men?"

Luke picked up where his boss was headed and smirked. "Women. Both of them."

"Shit, Luke. In that case, all it'll take is one of your movie-star grins, and they'll be putty in your hands, swooning where they stand while asking for your autograph."

Luke emitted one of those grins. "Well, then. Let's put it to the test, shall we?"

Inside the Ventura office, everyone in the bullpen greeted him with warm smiles and hellos. He'd spent the last four months with these people. He knew all of them and had worked with many of them. He'd expected nothing less from those special agents, but he'd gotten a different feeling upon his cursory introduction to Supervisory Senior Resident Agent Barbara Sutherlin. Luke was hoping it was because it was so brief, and also her first day—in truth, her first few minutes before she'd yet to enter her new office. *Guess we're gonna find out what she's really like.* Interestingly, meeting Assistant Resident Agent Debra Sines had been the exact opposite.

After Luke conducted a mass introduction of Dave to the Ventura agents, he asked if Agent Sutherlin was available. She must have heard his request, because at that second, she appeared at the bullpen doorway and waved him and Dave into her office. Her gesture, curt and aloof, blew toward them with an icy gust, giving the impression that any possible pleasantries weren't likely to be forthcoming. Once inside her personal space, Luke was uncomfortable, sorry to discover his first impression had been right.

Special Agent Sutherlin was an attractive fortyish-something woman—like early forties—with auburn hair in a chic, end-of-the-jaw cut. But contrary to her stoic expression, her eyes, a bright, glistening green—lighter and more brilliant than emeralds—radiated with what could only be described as ... *warmth?* She didn't smile, though, so it was hard to tell if what he thought he'd seen was real. The kindliness, if it had been there in the first place, was gone in an instant. She was all business and, to be honest, more than a tad snarky.

"You must be the other high and mighty DC replacement agent filling out the LA field office space next door," she said, regarding Dave with a narrow-eyed squint and a biting sting in her tone. "Since I've already met *him*," she flicked her head toward Luke, "I'm sure pretty boy here told you who I am and my position. Who are you?"

Dave handled the awkward moment and his introduction with consummate grace, for all the good it did him.

"Special Agent Dave Knapp, Phil Brooke's replacement as ASAC of Major Thefts," he said, holding out his hand. "Very nice to meet you, Special Agent Sutherlin."

Sutherlin didn't make a move to shake Dave's hand. "That's Supervisory Senior Resident Agent Sutherlin, *Mr.* Knapp," she hissed.

Stunned, Luke didn't know how he would've responded to the abrasive comment and was glad he didn't have to. In contrast, Dave didn't buckle, lose his poise, or so much as blink at the caustic remark.

"My apologies, *Supervisory Senior Resident Agent* Sutherlin," he said calmly and with a clear hint of humor. "I was under the impression all FBI agents carried the rank of *Special* Agent first and foremost. I was totally unaware you didn't make the grade."

Luke froze. *Did he really just say that?* He wanted nothing more than to swing a disbelieving glance at his boss, but he held back the urge, keeping his focus on the floor in front of him. To say the remark was cheeky would have been putting it mildly. More like downright rude. But then, Sutherlin had started it and definitely deserved the biting response—in his opinion, anyway.

In that moment, although he had no idea what would follow or how horribly this less-than-friendly meeting would screw up their relationship with their satellite office peers, Luke had nothing but admiration for his boss.

Within seconds, the corners of Sutherlin's mouth began turning up until she displayed a beautiful smile, which she coupled with a chuckle.

"Touché, Special Agent Knapp, and you can call me Barb." She shook Dave's hand and then Luke's as he extended it.

"And I'm Dave and this is Luke. Good to know we have LA savvy agents next door to help us navigate our step up from the DC crap-train to a Bureau system where we might actually get something done."

Oh ... Well done, David!

Barb dipped a nod. "I apologize for my brash facade. I always put on a hard shell for the agents I supervise when I first come in." She waved her hand toward the bullpen. "I believe in strict discipline, so I come into a new place with the reputation of being a leader no one wants to cross. For you two, it was a test. I can't tolerate bootlickers. I'm happy to have agents with some grit working next door." She leaned forward. "Can you keep a secret?"

The gesture and smirk on her face caught Luke off guard. *Is this woman bipolar?* Again, Dave came to the rescue.

"Absolutely."

She grinned. "After I've accomplished my goal, I'll let up on them."

"I had a teacher in school like that," Luke said with a laugh. "Ended up being my favorite because of the respect I and everyone else had for her."

"Exactly," Barb responded.

Okay. Not bipolar. Just needs a warm up with strangers.

"Now, let me introduce you to a new member of this satellite office, one I brought with me when I came over from White Collar in LA. Luke, you met her briefly last week when we arrived as you were leaving." She palmed the office phone's receiver and punched a couple buttons. "Deb, could you please come to my office?"

The approximate fifty-foot walk down and across the hall brought the agent to her destination, and Luke realized she was now sole owner of the guest office he had occupied while he was a visiting agent working the Pacific-Coast burglary case.

"This is Special Agent Debra Sines, the Ventura satellite office's new Assistant Resident Agent, my second in charge. It's a brand-new position I created here," Barb said. "Deb, meet the new Major Thefts ASAC, Special Agent Dave Knapp, or Dave, as he'd rather be called. You and I have already met Luke—Special Agent Luke Keltry, Supervisory Special Agent of the newest High-End Theft Unit—brief though our meeting was."

The tall, perky, thirty-year-old blond with the cutest pixie haircut and lustrous, platinum-gray eyes that seemed to dance with a glimmer of rascality greeted them cordially. She held Luke's gaze for a scant moment as she shook his hand before intensifying the eye-lock, but he didn't get the impression she was flirting. Her confident stare struck him as more of a ... challenge. Seemed peculiar, and on top of that, she took a step closer to him while casting her intriguing orbs on Dave. She swept glances between the two of them as she confirmed she also preferred the more casual "Deb" to any of the formalities the DC offices might impose.

"I think you may have a slightly misconstrued idea of what goes on in DC, formality-wise, among us commoners, anyway," Dave said. "But you're right about the higher-up muckety-mucks. Meetings with them tend to be unnecessarily stiff and proper—suit and tie proper. It's nice getting away from that."

"In that case, welcome to California and the world of generally laid-back FBI agents, chinos, and tank tops. Please do let us know if we can be of assistance to your transition." With that, Deb dipped her head and departed.

Luke's focus rested on her exit, perhaps longer than it should have, while he tried to make sense of the emotions she'd churned up. Why would she, an FBI agent holding a totally different position in a totally different Bureau office, feel the need to challenge him? She'd been friendly enough, for sure, but something unspoken was going on in that pretty little head of hers, and he had to admit, he'd give anything to find out what it was.

9

In the end, no one took on the job of pairing up the six Robin(s) for the "save the Vettes" operation. Because all the latest generation were well-versed in every aspect of high-end theft, they decided to keep it simple and draw names out of a bowl. Devon's idea, naturally. *Really high-tech, girlfriend.* Rayla restrained a giggle.

She paired with her two-year-older cousin, Wendy, Devon with Laura, and Tami with Krista. Rayla was excited, and not only to see "Vette Heaven" once again. She'd been to the Bowling Green Assembly Plant and the Corvette Museum a few times, but she hadn't had any proper one-on-one time with Wendy in quite a while. *Should be fun.*

After dinner, the five visiting Robin(s) checked into an Ann Arbor hotel to kick back for some down time while she returned home for her last evening with her parents. Camille and Eliot didn't know his cousin Tarry's daughters were in town. Better that way. Too many questions Rayla didn't want to answer, and Mom and Dad were busy finishing up their packing for Bangladesh, anyway.

She drove her parents to the airport at seven a.m. on Wednesday and bid them farewell for the first leg of their trip to the impoverished country that would be their home for the next two years. They'd be stopping off in Paris for a goodbye visit with Gram before catching their next flight out, an additional let-down for Rayla. That, by necessity, would prevent the Robin(s) of the Hood matriarch from traveling to

Cape Town to stake out The Contessa herself, though Rayla had no reason to believe Gram would do so even if she could. The woman hadn't indicated any such inclination.

With her parents gone, Rayla opened her family home to the Robin(s) for the remainder of their stay, and by Wednesday evening they had scoped out a plan and were ready to take down some very bad thieves—the kind that gave high-end theft a bad name. The ladies flew to Nashville and then took a hopper flight to Bowling Green Airport on Thursday.

All had quickly decided driving down wasn't a viable option. Besides none relishing the seven-hour trip, motoring down wouldn't leave much time to prepare. Flying allotted them significantly more opportunity to surveil and set up their sting.

Not that there was much to set up. If her five computer-savvy Robin(s) sisters had hacked proficiently, something Rayla never questioned, they knew almost every move the thieves planned to make. The only part of the heist for which they couldn't attain information was where the thieves were taking the cars once they'd stolen them. Therefore, the Robin(s) would need to position themselves in pairs around the GM Assembly Plant, watch the theft go down, then follow the thieves to their lair. Once there, one of them would call in the burglary with the appropriate amount of drama to get the local LEOs on site. Since the police would undoubtedly find Vettes or parts of them from the other states these guys had robbed yet to be shipped out, they would certainly call in the feds.

By the book. Piece of cake.

That was the plan and state of mind they all shared as they donned their thief gear and headed out of the hotel at the onset of darkness on Friday. And their plan was working great until they'd tailed the thieves to a private airfield north of Bowling Green shortly after midnight instead of a stationary destination—such as a warehouse doubling as a chop shop. Rayla looked on, stupefied. *What on earth?* As she and her cohorts watched from a safe distance, the low-life scumbags were driving the sleek sports cars up a cargo plane ramp. *They're flying the six Vettes they've just stolen to God only knows where.*

Change of plan.

"Devon, take out the plane's electrical systems before they can raise that ramp," Rayla instructed. Any one of the Robin(s) could have done it with a laptop, but Devon was the fastest.

"On it," Devon replied.

"As soon as you've done that, join the rest of us at the plane." She turned her attention to the other four Robin(s). "Ladies, I think it would be wise to wear hair up and facial masks for this one."

As everyone complied, she tapped 9-1-1 on her burner phone, the Robin(s) state-of-the-art voice-altering device securely covering the mouthpiece. When the operator answered, Rayla imparted the necessary information. "There's been a theft at the GM Assembly plant. The armed robbers are loading brand new Corvettes onto a cargo plane at the Boyd Airfield north of town. They're getting ready to take off, so you need to send every available law-enforcement unit to that field ASAP. This is not a crank call. The Robin(s) of the Hood are on site, keeping the thieves from taking off as long as possible, but law enforcement and SWAT need to mobilize quickly and get over here. As I stated, the thieves are armed and dangerous."

She waited for the operator to respond and listened for the young-sounding man to put out the call to the police. When he asked her to please stay on the line, she didn't end the call, but dropped the burner phone out the window. Then, she put her hair up and donned the three-quarter-face-covering, black, Zorro-style mask. By that time, Devon had taken out the plane's electrical systems, and the big gray monster stood dark on the runway. All six Robin(s) took off at a dead sprint for the back of the plane and up the ramp into the cargo hold.

Rayla knew her Vettes. All of these were latest model, 495 horsepower, mid-engine, 6.2 liter, V8, eight-speed, dual clutch C8s in six of the twelve available colors for the newest Stingray design. A closer look revealed they were the 3LT models, and the front splitters and specific wing spoilers confirmed they carried the Z51 Package—the necessary addition to achieve the mind-blowing zero to sixty mph in under three seconds. She swiftly chose the car closest to the ramp, the Torch Red "Ray," featuring black metallic trim— which flared from the side vent fin to form the invisible outside door handle and RPO wing spoiler, standard from the factory. Opening the unlocked door, she stared inside to see the Jet Black/Red Trim, 3LT-specific interior.

Yes, she noticed. She took in every inch of the phenomenal vehicle. Being in the middle of a heisting challenge didn't affect her ability to appreciate a beautiful piece of machinery ... especially these latest model Vettes.

While the rest of the Robin(s) each chose another of the six cars, the group began talking through their earbuds, working to figure out how to move the vehicles. The engines were equipped with keyless entry and start buttons, but without the key-fobs, none of them had any conception as to how they'd get them out.

Rayla strained her brain for an answer. These high-powered technical wonders couldn't be hot-wired. Rayla knew the Vette's brand-new gear lever buttons wouldn't do squat without the car running. *So, no putting them in neutral and pushing.* With the cargo plane dark, they needed to get a move on before the thieves were onto them. *But how?*

As soon as she positioned herself behind the semi-square, "squircle" steering wheel, Rayla pushed the start button. Like an answer from heaven, the Vette roared to life. *The fobs must be somewhere close by. Maybe the guys up front have them?* She robotically checked the passenger compartment and saw the smart-key fob lying inside. The others confirmed the same, and five more engines started in quick succession. *Very accommodating of these thieves to leave the fobs inside the cars.*

Rayla backed the Torch Red Stingray down the ramp at a pretty good clip. Laura followed in the Sebring Orange Ray, Krista in the Accelerate Yellow, Tami in the Rapid Blue, Wendy in the Arctic White, and Devon in the Blade Silver, all speeding down the cargo plane ramp in reverse as if they were racing in the Indie 500. But Devon hadn't completely cleared the ramp before the six thugs appeared, guns drawn, all in black with either ski masks or balaclavas covering their faces. There was little doubt the beasties were angry, and even less they wouldn't blink an eye before killing any one of them.

As Devon sped down the ramp, one thug took aim, but another, probably the head of the operation, pushed the man's gun down before a shot was fired. Rayla couldn't hear the conversation over the engines, but she could imagine what was being said. Head-honcho guy clearly had some brains. He didn't want the C8s marred. This was good news, which the Robin(s) could use to their advantage. As long as they stayed inside the Vettes, the thugs wouldn't shoot at them.

"They won't risk damaging the cars, ladies," Rayla said. "Go right at them and bump them off with your car."

With that command, five dazzling Stingrays easily ran down and took out five of the armed thugs. With a sudden stroke of genius, Rayla let the sixth guy get away. "Devon, reinstate the electrical systems for the plane."

While the other Robin(s) zip tied the thieves they'd immobilized—hands and feet—piling their guns a good distance away, Rayla drove her Vette back up the ramp.

Inside, she stealthily exited her Stingray as Devon responded to her request with notable swiftness. The sixth thief, who also happened to be head-honcho guy, did exactly what Rayla expected: boarded the plane, fired it up, and began closing the ramp door. Before the door completely closed,

Rayla tagged the inside of the plane with a long-range GPS device.

Mission accomplished, she leapt to freedom in the nick of time as the escaping thief began taxiing and the plane's cargo door slammed shut. Seconds after liftoff, dozens of police cars drove onto the scene, sirens blasting and their blue and white lights flashing like an out of sync light show.

Tami informed the others she'd stuffed a Robin(s) calling card into a thug's mouth, and Rayla dropped the other half of the tracking transmitter on top of the guns as they all ducked out of sight.

Once they were safe in their dark, well-hidden vehicle, Devon hacked into the police radio frequency and informed the cops of the tracker Rayla planted which would allow them to follow the one un-rescued Stingray and probably find a worthwhile stash of other Corvettes and/or parts from the nationwide car thefts.

They hung around until the police wrapped up, wanting to watch and listen in via their computer hack-in, but also not willing to risk being seen as they drove away. On their way back to the hotel, they took turns helping each other change out of their black leather. Laura, who had been driving, pulled over to let Krista take the wheel so she could change. No way they wanted to risk showing up at a small-town hotel dressed like the thieves they were. As they drove, they chattered excitedly about what they had accomplished.

Back at the hotel, they gathered in one room to watch the footage of their bust running on an Internet site—and it was great news. Not only had the Bowling Green PD, County Mounties, and Kentucky State Police picked up the five thieves the Robin(s) had tied up in a bow for them, but the FBI were notified and had used the GPS the Robin(s) provided to track the plane. The feds had located the vile chop shop in northern Georgia, finding various parts along with a few Corvettes still intact, from all the robberies across the Midwest. Agents from the FBI Atlanta field office had rounded up the rest of the gang, twelve gun-yielding thieves in all, and arrested the pilot as soon as he deplaned.

During his emotional multimedia statement, the Bowling Green Chief of Police went so far as to thank the Robin(s) of the Hood, an unprecedented compliment and recognition, for their part in bringing the "Corvette Gang" to justice.

As they toasted their success with champagne, Rayla drinking sparkling water because of her alcohol aberration, Devon's face crinkled in a sly grin. "Just how difficult was it for you to drive that Stingray back onto the plane and leave it and all the other Vettes we rescued for the cops, Ray?"

Rayla's tightened lips split wide open with uncontrollable mirth. "You have no idea!"

10

"MAN, I MISSED YOU," Luke whispered, nuzzling her neck as he puffed his warm breath into her ear.

Her back nestled snuggly against his firm, muscular form, Rayla rolled to her side to face him and scooched closer. "I missed you, too. You know we were apart for a whole four days?" She snickered.

"Go ahead. Make fun of me. I still missed you. This bed may as well have been a prison cot without you in here with me."

"You say the sweetest things, love." She moved to kiss him but stopped short, her lips barely brushing his. "How would you know what a prison cot feels like? Part of your FBI training? Like you have to spend a night or maybe a weekend in the clink to understand all aspects of criminals and what you're supposed to make their final destination?"

He slid his hand from her waist to palm her face, his fingers lightly skimming her back along their journey. His large maple-syrup eyes were close enough for her to feel the butterfly kisses his long lashes delivered to her brow, and she quivered with the unexpected ecstasy the feathery wisps transmitted. Then he kissed her, and ecstasy didn't begin to describe the passion that flowed like a newly undammed river throughout her entire body.

Momentarily, he eased his lips from hers a tiny fraction. "I have no idea what a prison cot feels like, sweetness. And, although spending time in jail wasn't on the FBI training docket, to my knowledge, prisoners get bunkbeds not cots, anyway. I just can't imagine it being any worse than what I felt without you here."

The kissing resumed, and as a result, she and Luke didn't make it out of bed for another hour.

After the Vette job had wrapped up, all the Robin(s) had flown out of Nashville around noon on Saturday. The approximately six-and-a-half-hour flight with one stopover in Dallas had landed them in Santa Barbara at around three-forty Pacific Time. Rayla caught a ride home with Devon, who lived in the same condo complex, and she and Luke were in each other's arms by four-thirty. Other than a break for dinner, they hadn't separated again the entire night, the eight hours sleep spent intertwined in each other's arms. Luke appeared sexually insatiable, and so was she … to a point. But she had something else splitting her attention, and he called her on it when they finally rolled out of bed.

"The Corvette thieves' capture and the Robin(s)' involvement is all over the news. No reason you can't tell me about it now, is there?" he asked as he zipped his jeans.

"Like you said, it's all over the news. I don't think there's much more I can add to what you've already seen."

He rounded the bed to sit beside her. "You're usually a lot more excited after a job, be it Robin(s) of the Hood or *Thief à la Femme*. But, you're not excited at all. As a matter of fact, I'd go so far as to say you're depressed. Want to tell me what went wrong?"

She cast her gaze onto his concerned features and shrugged. "Nothing went wrong. We got a bit of a surprise and had to deviate from our original plan when we saw the thieves loading the Stingrays onto a cargo plane, but we scrambled with our usual efficiency and got the job done."

"So, what's with the long face? I have better than average powers of observation, babe, but honestly, anyone could see you're upset about something."

Again, she shrugged. She wasn't willing to tell him about The Triple Crown thefts, at least not yet. While wracking her brain to come up with an excuse for her troubled consternation, Luke bailed her out.

"I'm guessing you saw the chop shop the FBI found because of your GPS tag on that cargo plane. Is that it? Are you in mourning for the Vettes you couldn't save?"

She took a deep breath and, pouncing on the opportunity to use the misdirection, she bit down on her lower lip and nodded with a pouty face.

Luke took her in his arms and kissed the top of her head. "You did everything you could, Rayla. Bad things happen when low-life thieves are involved. You saved six classic, just-manufactured Stingrays and several other not yet disassembled Corvettes from the warehouse in Georgia. Take the win."

She laid her head in the crook of his neck. "Thanks, love." She felt bad about lying to him, but it wasn't entirely a lie. She hated they hadn't caught the Vette thugs sooner, but that wasn't the uneasiness that consumed her now.

As she'd feared and predicted, The Contessa of Kimberley had been stolen in the early hours of Saturday morning, September 12th—right on schedule to complete the second leg of The Triple Crown challenge—despite the anonymous heads-up tip she'd phoned in to the Cape Town police.

The first news of the South African theft broke after she'd gone to bed while in Kentucky. She knew because she'd scoured the Internet for it before turning in at around three a.m. Saturday. Since there had been no news of the theft at that time, she had drifted into a restful sleep with renewed hope she'd been wrong about the Lynx theft linking to the heisting challenge.

The first thing she had done when she woke was grab her laptop and search again. And there it was. The theft of The Contessa of Kimberley had been perpetrated flawlessly—the way a really good high-end thief or thieves would do it—with no trace of the burglar left behind. The one-hundred-twelve carat Brilliant Cushion-shape diamond was gone without any way to trail it, precisely the same as the Lynx had been stolen a week earlier. Since there had been no mention of a police stakeout, or any extra security placed on the gem, clearly her warning phone call had fallen on deaf ears.

Upon reading the report, she'd fleetingly entertained the possibility the thieves had been stealing The Contessa while she and the Robin(s) were taking down the Vette thugs. But after thinking through it, she realized that likely had not been the case. The curator found the diamond gone when he'd opened the museum at nine a.m. South African Standard Time—seven hours ahead of the U.S. Eastern Time Zone. Much more logical the gem had been lifted in Cape Town while she and the Robin(s) had enjoyed an early dinner in Bowling Green, Kentucky—several hours before their tête-à-tête with the Vette thieves.

Her worst fear confirmed, she hadn't left the bed before she'd called her grandmother, whom she'd intended to scold for her lack of concern. But, rather than a defensive posture and an attempt to console Rayla, Gram had been the one who needed consoling.

She'd been there. At the Cape Town Diamond Museum. The Robin(s) matriarch had put Rayla on "Rescue the Corvettes" duty while she'd taken it upon herself to stake out The Contessa. Only she'd arrived too late. Eliot and Camille's visit coupled with a snafu renting a vehicle at the Cape Town airport set her back, enough for her to miss the entire theft. According to Gram, the burglary must have occurred at or shortly after midnight, because when she arrived around twelve-thirty, the diamond display was already vacant, and the thief or thieves were nowhere to be found. Gram couldn't even figure out how they'd done it. She'd said it was as if the gem had just disappeared. This was up there as one of, if not *the* best executed theft she'd ever *not* witnessed. And she couldn't stop apologizing to Rayla.

At that point, Rayla confirmed she'd thought about letting the other Robin(s) from ARI handle the Corvette theft sting, allowing her to slip away to Cape Town, but she couldn't do it. "You were right to give me that job, Gram," she'd said. "The Vettes captured my attention more so than The Contessa of Kimberley diamond ever could. I had to help. This isn't your fault. I would have negated your wishes and gone to Cape Town if the job you assigned me had been anything but Vettes."

That got a small chuckle from Gram.

"But with my help or not, I know if you had been there while the theft was going down, you would have stopped it."

The moment of amusement she'd tugged from her grandmother vanished too soon. Nothing could erase the grief the woman touted for her inability to save The Contessa or the ongoing concern for the next and last diamond in line: The Maiden of St. Marys.

Rayla was aware—because of ARI's trolling of the dark web, as well as the FBI and Interpol's intelligence networks—that the Robin(s) had a full schedule of various heists around the country to perpetrate in the coming week. All were thefts which would bring justice to innocent individuals who needed their help. So, when Gram gave her the go-ahead to tackle The Triple Crown threat as *Thief à la Femme*, it came as no surprise. However, her grandmother's last words caused a lump to form in her throat.

"I'm sure you can do a better job of protecting The Maiden than I did protecting The Contessa, dear. I trust you won't let me down the way I have you."

Nothing more she'd said had appeased the woman, and after many tries, Rayla finally allowed Gram to end the call. But she hadn't wasted a minute contacting her number one— well, her only—diamond forger. If he could fashion a forgery for her relatively quickly, she had an idea for protecting The Maiden. He was more than happy to help her.

Game on.

She lifted her head from where it nestled in her boyfriend's neck and dug into her grifting bag of tricks to give him a positive smile. He'd been so sweet, trying to comfort her for something for which she hadn't needed comforting. Now she'd have to keep up the lie, tell him she'd be leaving on another mission for the Robin(s), most likely by mid-week, when in fact she was breaking their pact and sneaking out without his knowledge as *Femme*. Because no matter what else was going on, one thing was certain: *Thief à la Femme* was going back to Michigan—beautiful upper Michigan and specifically Mackinac Island and its Grand Hotel—to foil the third leg of The Triple Crown of Jewel Theft

11

FULLY AWARE OF RAYLA'S flight out for a Robin(s) mission early Wednesday morning, as well as the fact two more Robin(s), Patti and Tarry, were in town for another of the sisterhood's clandestine operations which would keep Rayla busy until late Tuesday, Luke waffled with SSRA Sutherlin's invitation for a social gathering. Barb, along with Deb and Dave, stood in his office, attempting to convince him of the fun it would be to have the heads and their significant others from the LA field office and the Ventura satellite office meet for dinner sometime in the coming week. Dave had been pressing him to meet Rayla, and now all three converged on him for a date and time.

It's not even eleven a.m. on a frickin' Monday morning. Give me a break. He was on the cusp of telling them scheduling would have to wait until Rayla returned from her *business* trip because he didn't know how long she'd be gone, when his lovely girlfriend, Tarry Santimore-Tett, and Patti Nichol-Sanders walked in.

To say he was stunned would have been a gross understatement. Rayla had never visited him at his FBI office, and to waltz in with two other Robin(s) of the Hood? *Chutzpa, ladies. I'll give you that.* Since Rayla had brought two members of the thieving sisterhood, one middle and one older generation, he had an inkling they needed his help or input on some job and were using the excuse of taking him to lunch to ask their favor. But what happened next hit him like a blast of snow in the face during a north-country snowstorm—the kind that takes your breath away.

Barb and Tarry knew each other. And if that wasn't enough of the already "it's a small world" happenstance, Luke swore he saw recognition in both Barb and Patti's eyes when they connected, as well.

Barb's explanation that she and Tarry went to school together would have appeased him if not for the momentary acknowledgement he swore he saw between Patti and Barb. There was no relational connection between Tarry and Patti. Yes, Tarry was Evie's niece and Patti Evie's best friend. But, since Patti was one of the original Robin(s) matriarchs—now an extremely robust, attractive, and feisty sixty-two, who had lived in Malibu most of her life—and the alluring, blond-haired, blue-eyed Tarry, and her long lost friend, Barb, were forty-two and had grown up in Miami, the chances Barb would know Patti seemed extremely unlikely.

He rarely second-guessed his initial observations, and he wasn't inclined to start now. Something was off.

Granted, he'd been super sensitive to Robin(s) of the Hood intel Rayla had been feeding him since he'd grilled Evie that day at the airport and she'd told him about his girlfriend's obsession with the diamond stolen in Norway. The reason for his keen sensitivity? Evie said Rayla wanted to track down the thief and return the diamond, that stealing that gem was one of the most contemptable thefts that could be perpetrated. So why hadn't Rayla mentioned it to him? That struck him as odd.

There were lots of thieves stealing lots of gems all over the world. It was the norm in his and Rayla's realm. What was so special about this diamond? Why would the theft of a seemingly inconsequential gem get her so riled? *And why won't she tell me?*

When he'd posed that question to Evie, she seemed evasive, eventually telling him it was a diamond she had taken Rayla to see as a young girl. She'd said she supposed Rayla had developed a fondness for it, and because the Robin(s) stole only from insidiously rich, low-life criminals preying on the innocent, the theft of The Levanger Lynx was one Rayla undoubtedly had found difficult to accept. She had no answer for Rayla's silence on the subject.

He hadn't spoken to Evie since that morning in Detroit, but after he'd learned about the Corvette operation, he wondered if this diamond somehow held the same place in Rayla's heart as had the Vettes she'd rescued. He decided then to find out as much as he could about the theft of the gem, but he had yet to find the time.

Barb knowing both Tarry and Patti struck him as a step beyond coincidental. Connected or not, he vowed to make the time to research the diamond from Norway. At this moment, however, he had enough to deal with right here in his office. His dazed focus drifted to Rayla as she made the introductions.

"I guess Luke's a little preoccupied, so permit me to introduce myself. I'm Rayla, and these two beautiful ladies are my Grandaunt Patti and my Aunt Tarry. They're in town visiting and wanted to meet Luke. I thought I'd surprise him..." she planted her irresistible sapphire gaze on Dave, "...and maybe you would allow us to take him for an early lunch?"

Luke snapped to attention. "Apologies. I'm a little out of it today. Rayla, Tarry, and Patti, allow me to introduce you to my direct superior, ASAC of LA's Major Thefts, Special Agent Dave Knapp, and the two ladies are the head and assistant head of the FBI Ventura satellite office next door: Supervisory Senior Resident Agent Barb Sutherlin and Assistant Resident Agent Deb Sines."

Handshakes and "how do you dos?" in process, Luke found a second to lock his questioning gaze into Rayla's amused one while his mind did wind sprints searching for answers to all this mystifying hoopla. *Grandaunt? Patti isn't her grandmother's sister.* A second's deliberation provided a likely explanation. Easier for Rayla to link the two ladies relationally, thus diffusing additional questions. *Sincerely brilliant. Except for Barb.* Since she knew them, Barb had to know Tarry and Patti were not mother and daughter.

Dave brought Luke's surmising to a grinding halt. "Very nice to meet you, ladies." He stepped closer to Rayla and extended his hand. "Especially nice to finally meet you, Rayla." After the handshake, he said, "Luke is the supervisor of his own unit. He doesn't need my permission to take an early or extended lunch, but ... since you asked..." He eyed Luke with a grin. "Go ahead. Take an early lunch and all the time you need."

The glint in Dave's eyes belied the supposed goodwill. His boss's unnecessary but allegedly kind gesture had been offered as a way to get him to talk more about his girlfriend, and now her family, too. Luke knew Dave's MO; the man wasn't going to give up digging, especially now that he'd finally met Rayla. *Her unannounced visit with two more of the Robin(s) might very well end my career and land the entire sisterhood in jail—with me in there next to them.* No exaggeration. Dave was that good of an investigator.

Luke extended an insincere smile. "Thanks, *boss*," he said. He turned to address Rayla and her ... *relatives*. "I'll meet you in the parking lot in a few minutes. I have a couple issues I need to wrap up first."

With a "nice meeting you all" punctuating their exit, the three Robin(s) left, Barb and Deb right behind them.

In the parking lot, Luke climbed into the SUV Tarry had rented. Before his behind hit the seat, he lasered his gaze into Rayla's and fired out his admonishment. "What the hell were you thinking? What on earth possessed you to show up here, and with two other Robin(s), too?" He released Rayla from his eye-lock and scanned Tarry and Patti in the front seat, eventually planting his focus on the former. "And the Supervisory Senior Resident Agent of the FBI's Ventura satellite office knows you? Great. How much does she know about you? She certainly seemed to know Patti, too."

They all started talking at once, and Luke raised his hand. When silence replaced their chattering, he said, "Rayla, you shouldn't have come without asking me first, but what's done is done. To help me get ahead of and deal with possible fallout, I need to know what the story is on Barb Sutherlin, or whatever her last name was back when you knew her," he said, returning his attention to Tarry.

"It was Sutherlin. She kept her maiden name when she married, and ... I'm sorry, Luke. It's the worst news possible. She was a thief back then. She worked with us, the then six members of the Robin(s), a couple of times. That's how she and Patti know each other." She cocked her head with her next introspective query. "You picked up on that? You saw recognition when Barb and Patti's eyes met?"

"He's an exceptional agent, Aunt Tarry," Rayla quipped.

He ignored the question and Rayla's response. "The Robin(s) are purely matriarchal. How did she come to work with you? To my knowledge you don't take on hired help."

"We were like twenty, sophomores in college at the University of Miami, when we met, became friends, and discovered our thieving connection. So, I asked Evie's permission and she granted Barb the privilege of working a couple jobs with us. Barb knew she couldn't join, but after getting a taste of our brand of theft, you know, the justice for others angle, she went out on her own doing that for a while. We kept in touch, and she and I did a couple of jobs together on the sly when I was sent out alone for the Robin(s). After graduation, she told me she was going to law school. After that, I lost touch with her. I was shocked beyond belief to see her here. She obviously decided to leave the Robin(s) alone, just like you, because I'm sure she easily could have tracked me down once she became an FBI agent. I stayed in Miami."

Tarry's features morphed to angst. "What do you know about her? Is she likely to change her mind now?"

"I don't know squat about her, at least not anything that would answer that question. She's the brand-new head of the Ventura satellite office and she came over from fifteen years in LA's White-Collar Division. That's all I know."

"If she was in White Collar for all those years, wouldn't she have been in the perfect position to track us down and arrest us?" Tarry asked.

"Yes," he answered. "The fact she didn't tells me she has no beef with the Robin(s) of the Hood, and she's not likely to go after you now. If she does, she's got to know it'll end her career, too, with your knowledge of her past."

They all jumped a little, startled by Barb rapping on the driver's door. Tarry turned the key and opened the window.

"I'm guessing you've talked things through enough to realize we have a bit of a sticky situation going on here, so I'd like to invite myself to lunch," Barb said with a wry smile. "I think we need to get this all out in the open and iron out the wrinkles."

Luke dropped his face in his hands, and Rayla laid her soft hand on his arm. "Starting to appreciate the fact prisons have those bunk beds instead of cots, hon?" she jibed. Her playful tone tugged a grin out of him.

He lifted his head and worked up a sardonic smile for the SSRA. "Why don't you come to lunch with us, Barb? As a matter of fact, I insist."

12

QUESTIONS AND FEAR saturated Luke as Tarry drove to the prearranged meeting site for lunch, and Barb followed in her own car. Finally, seated at a secluded picnic table in an abandoned park on the outskirts of town—with the five younger generation Robin(s) present as well—Luke's first question pummeled Barb with the force of a tsunami. "Why did you assume I knew who these ladies were?"

The agent's answer was preceded by a chuckle and a dismissive wave of her hand. "Same way you saw the recognition between Patti and me, I presume. FBI training, and we're damn good at our jobs. Anyway, I was fairly sure you had all the skinny. You're a sharp agent, Keltry, as is your boss. I assume he knows, too?"

"No!" Every member of the Robin(s) crew, as well as Luke, answered at the same time and with equal intensity. Then, they laughed.

"Dave's not in the loop on this one, and it's really important he stay that way," Luke said. "I consider my boss a friend, but Dave has FBI blood running in his veins. I'm not at all convinced he would, or even could, agree to keep this secret. Besides, these ladies step ever closer to being outed with every individual who becomes privy."

"How did you get them to accept you?" she asked. Scanning the group at the table, she pitched her next question at them. "I mean, at some point you found out he was a federal agent. I would have thought you'd have scattered as soon as you knew."

"That's a long story," Rayla said. "Suffice it to say, Luke's and my relationship played a big part, and Luke agreed to a lot of rules."

"As did you," Luke inserted.

Barb continued her perusal of the table's occupants. "You younger ladies are the latest generation. Care to fill in the blanks, Tarry?"

After Tarry introduced Barb to the five youngest Robin(s) she had yet to meet, complete with whose daughters they were, and brought the agent up to speed on Rayla's inclusion as Evie's granddaughter, Barb gave them the assurance they'd all hoped for. She was no threat to them or their cause. She never had been and never would be.

"The Robin(s) are the reason I became an FBI agent," she said, much to everyone's surprise. "It's true. After tagging along with Tarry, I got a taste for the type of theft your sisterhood perpetrated, and I guess there were some good morals buried underneath that larcenous nature of mine. I couldn't go back to stealing as a career meant to make me rich. I thought briefly about trying to put together my own group, but I soon realized the pointlessness in that effort. The Robin(s) of the Hood are unique among thieves—making a good living from taking down the worst criminals while providing justice for those who can't obtain it legally. Finding other trained thieves willing to do what you do was an impractical undertaking, and training my own crew wasn't any more realistic. The FBI provided me with the perfect solution. I pretty much do what you do, but from the other side of the law."

Her brow furrowed, and her eyes flitted back and forth a couple times with the statement before she added, "Not exactly the same, I know. But it works for me."

"I thought you became a lawyer," Tarry said. "Your enrollment in law school was the last thing we talked about."

"Oh ... yeah ... *that*. I made it a semester before I found out what the word boring truly means." After a gurgling laugh, she continued, "I've followed all the press on you gals. You're a credit to the planet. I thought so then, and I haven't changed my opinion."

Luke cleared his throat. "I have to believe your intention to keep their secret extends to me, as well? Outing me as a compromised agent would entail breaking your promise to them."

"That's right," Barb replied. "And it works the other way, too. Although I was never arrested, I was a thief at one time. I'm fairly sure that would get me thrown out of the Bureau ... at the very least. We have every reason to keep each other's secrets, Luke." She smiled at the women. "If memory serves, only four of you are missing today: Evie, Katherine, Amy, and Jodi. Is that right?"

"Good memory," Tarry responded. "There would have been nine of us at this point if Evie hadn't brought Rayla in and allowed me to bring in all three of my daughters. She was happy to have the extra 'girl power,' thought twelve sounded like a good round number."

As they dug into the bucket of chicken and sides the younger Robin(s) had bought for the picnic, chattering away as women everywhere did, Luke stole a reciprocating eye-lock with Rayla, and they knew the other's thoughts. No one had mentioned Rayla being *Thief à la Femme*, and none would. That was extra intel Barb didn't need, and definitely not information any of them wanted her to have.

Having eaten and given the sisterhood his promise to provide them with the background they needed for a certain low-life insurance agent, back at the office, Luke wrapped up everything he needed to do earlier than anticipated. That accomplishment opened the perfect opportunity for him to finally look into The Levanger Lynx robbery.

The news link he clicked on, which had recently been updated, provided an abundance of information on the rock from Norway, sufficient for what he needed or wanted to know. But he soon discovered there was more to this than one stolen diamond. Since The Levanger Lynx theft, there had been another burglary—a one-hundred-twelve carat gem, The Contessa of Kimberley, on display in South Africa—and the two thefts had an ominous connection. Another link within the body of the article snared his attention as if it were highlighted in flashing neon orange and jumping off the page in 3-D.

Swiftly clicking on the link, what he found in the accompanying article floored him. *The Levanger Lynx and this Contessa are two diamonds in a three-diamond heisting challenge?* The third gem, The Maiden of St. Marys, according to the challenge rules, was due to be lifted this coming Saturday. He swallowed hard with the next bit of intel. *In Michigan.*

Luke stared at the information about the third diamond on his computer screen, soaking it in as he jotted down a few key words and symbols on the corner of his desk pad's calendar, and attempted to make sense of it—specifically how it likely involved Rayla.

In the world of high-end theft, this diamond linked to the other two in what was known as The Triple Crown. No one had ever pulled it off; not stealing all three in the necessary succession and on their distinctive dates, anyway.

The Triple Crown. Like the horse-racing Triple Crown. Three events taking place, or needing to take place, on specific days. *Except these are jewel heists, not horse races.*

He remembered Rayla telling him about the vacations she and her parents took to Mackinac Island every summer, and, specifically, her description of the "superlative" diamond affixed in a chandelier at the top of the hotel. *The Maiden of St. Marys.* Rayla had rattled on and on about the gem one evening while he tuned out the details of her musing, rather focusing on the way her eyes—hell, her whole countenance—lit up as she described the diamond in perfect detail.

There's no way she's not involved in these thefts, and no way she's not going after the last diamond. But something about that conclusion didn't add up or make sense. They had a pact. She'd agreed to stick to his rules about what she would steal as *Femme.* This was a fifty-year-old challenge she must have known about before she'd met him. *So why would she take on this challenge now? Is she thumbing her nose at me?*

A moment's more thought presented a much more feasible likelihood. Rayla had been in Virginia with him at Josh's wedding when the first gem had been stolen. She couldn't have done it. He knew the youngest generation Robin(s) had been in Kentucky when The Contessa was stolen a week later. Was it possible Rayla wasn't with them? *No, she would have wanted to be involved in taking down Vette thieves.* Besides, if she hadn't stolen the first diamond, there was no reason for her to steal the next two. The challenge rules were very clear.

That meant his larcenous girlfriend was upset about the thefts. She wasn't a "steal from good, honest people" sort of thief anyway; of that much, he was certain. Evie said Rayla loved the Lynx. It was much more likely she was distressed to learn it had been stolen. That's what he'd seen in her beautiful yet conflicted face when she'd watched the footage of that theft on the news at her mom and dad's place. *And I'll bet my badge she was equally distraught about The Contessa's theft when I thought she was mourning the Vettes she couldn't rescue. If she was that upset about the first two, she must be beside herself with the thought of someone stealing The Maiden.*

He jolted with his next thought. *She's leaving on Wednesday morning, but not on a Robin(s) job. She's going on a mission to save the diamond in Michigan ... solo ... as Thief à la Femme.*

From everything he'd learned about Rayla over the last three months he'd been involved with her, he knew he was right. *The question is ... what am I going to do about it?*

13

Rayla had never been more grateful than she was today for the rules the Robin(s) had imposed on Luke when her FBI boyfriend wriggled his way into their inner circle. Technically, she was using a Robin(s) rule for what was a *Femme* undertaking, but that was inconsequential—at least to her. As far as she was concerned, *Femme* and the Robin(s) were interchangeable, but Luke didn't see it that way. He was better off not knowing she'd be operating alone for her upcoming job. That particular rule, the one that stated he couldn't know anything about the Robin(s)' missions unless they were working for him, served her very well today.

He must have asked her three times if he could drive her to the airport, phrasing it slightly differently with every query. She patiently reminded him: "You can't know where I'm headed or what alias I'm using to get there. This assignment isn't connected to the one Patti and Aunt Tarry brought you in for. Gram's sending me on a different mission." That much was true. "Therefore, it's out of your purview." According to Luke's pact with her as *Thief à la Femme*, that was *not* true. "I'm sorry, hon. I'm not allowed to tell you anything, including the mode of transportation I'm using to get there." She completed the string of lies by throwing her hands in the air as if she were as upset about it as he was.

"You're just going to leave your Vette in long-term parking at some airport for five or more days? Aren't you worried about it?" He took her hands in his. "Why don't we switch rides for this week. You take my truck and I'll babysit your Vette."

"Oh, right," she said with a laugh. "So you can track me via your truck's GPS? I don't think so, sweetheart. And who said I'm flying, anyway? Thanks for the offer, but I'm leaving my Vette here. Devon's driving me." Rayla knew Luke easily could track her Vette and Devon's BMW, and if he were inclined to do so, he'd find out in a hurry: Neither vehicles were travelling to any airports.

She'd leave the condo complex with Devon's help, but an Uber would collect her at the bus station for her trip to LAX. Luke didn't know the alias she'd be using for this job; she herself didn't know it yet. Her BFF would be delivering the newly forged documents when she picked her up, direct from Patti. Because of that, with all the Ubers and taxis waiting at and coming and going from the bus station, not to mention the possibility she'd have taken the bus, there was no way Luke could know how she'd left town or where she was headed unless he followed her. She was fairly sure he wouldn't. He knew she was too good not to spot him, and she'd definitely be on the lookout for him.

She'd gone to an exorbitant amount of trouble to make sure he couldn't track her, but she'd learned to be thorough when Luke was involved. For some reason, he seemed overly suspicious about this supposed Robin(s) job. *It's like he knows I'm doing an off-book Femme thing.* How or why he suspected her dishonesty was anyone's guess. She was a consummate liar.

Their last kiss and goodbye hug completed, bittersweet though it was, Luke left for his office an hour earlier than usual—another reason why she had been suspicious of his intentions. He said he had a lot of paperwork to catch up on, but might he be planning to lie in wait, hell-bent on following her? She'd have to deal with that possibility when Devon picked her up.

After watching him drive away from the lanai window, she returned to the master bedroom to resume packing, replacing the summertime items she'd originally chosen with warmer fall clothing for her Upper Michigan "save The Maiden" operation.

She'd purposely begun arranging warm weather clothing, including a bikini, inside her carryon bag and then concealed the luggage, knowing Luke had been watching when she'd "surreptitiously" stashed it. She'd expected the astute FBI agent to take note of her attempt to hide the bag, certain that would prompt him to look inside. For sure, that would lead her nosy boyfriend in the wrong direction if he continued on his quest to ascertain her destination.

Burglary equipment stowed within a lead-lined, false compartment sewed into the bottom of her extra-large luggage to be checked at the airport—with clothing and various other items packed in such a way as to obscure it—and all else fitted snugly in her carryon bag, Rayla emptied all ID cards from her wallet and purse. Devon arrived as she finished, and the two hauled her bags to her friend's black BMW i8 coup and set out for the bus station in Santa Barbara.

As soon as they were on the road, Devon handed her a small manila envelope of forged documents for the mission— what amounted to $500 cash, a California driver's license, two credit cards, and a health insurance card—all bearing the name Claire Annabel Sanford.

As usual, Patti's forgeries were exceptional. No one would look twice or bat an eye when any of these IDs were presented. The credit cards were set up to function as genuine accounts. The places she'd use them wouldn't realize they weren't getting paid until a day after she left when the accounts would be removed without a trace … compliments of Devon's badass hacking.

When they arrived at the Greyhound Bus Station, Rayla waved down a random Uber. While the driver loaded her bags in the trunk, she and Devon hugged their goodbyes, and moments later, after a careful scan to make sure she wasn't followed, Rayla was on her way to LA. There, she caught a non-stop flight to Detroit followed by a private flight she'd chartered, which would take her directly to St. Ignace, Michigan.

Luke knew he'd pushed the issue of driving Rayla to the airport more than he should have, so much so he was sure he'd made her suspicious. His crafty girlfriend picked up on the slightest deceitful nuances, be it tone of voice or peculiar eye movements. He thought he'd passed those tests, but for sure she'd zeroed in on his continued attempts to garner information about how and where she was going. His excessive pressing made following her a useless option. She'd be watching for that.

It didn't matter, though. He was sure she was on her way to Michigan, and it was a forgone conclusion she'd be flying, and that under a fake name. After enlisting Moneypenny, his Chevy Colorado's personalized Intellilink System sweetheart, to check flight schedules to Michigan out of Santa Barbara and Los Angeles while he drove to Ventura, he concluded Rayla was undoubtedly booked on the ten-a.m. non-stop flight out of LAX into Detroit. From there, she'd likely booked another flight north, or possibly chartered a flight right onto Mackinac Island. *So, all I have to do is contrive a reasonable excuse for me to go there.* Right. *How the hell am I going to do that?*

So, color him surprised when he arrived at the office to find a computer printout of a Michigan State Police seminar dealing with how to spot all manner of forgeries taking place at Grand Hotel on Mackinac Island the following day through Saturday lying on his chair. Dave filled in the gaps.

"As head of the High-End Theft Unit in DC, I attended a forgery seminar early on, and I found it very helpful. HETU normally deals with straight up theft, but as you know, every once in a while, forgery plays into the mix. I think you can benefit from this seminar as head of the west coast HETU, if you're up to traveling back to Michigan. Turns out, Mackinac Island, and specifically Grand Hotel with its many conference facilities, has fielded police and FBI seminars every fall for many years. I was thrilled on your behalf to see this one and to find it was a forgery conference this year. The MSP is bringing in our very own FBI specialist, Special Agent Charles Milford, who is a well-known top dog in this area, both in the intelligence community and police departments all over the country." His grin was more of a knowing smirk. "Since Michigan is where Rayla's from, and Mackinac Island is considered a romantic vacation spot, I figure you can make it a getaway with her, as well. What do you say?"

Though it seemed an uncanny coincidence for this convention to drop in his lap, Luke was sure his face had lit up. Sure, it was the last thing he expected, but life had been smiling on him lately. *Who am I to look a gift horse in the mouth?* "Uh, yeah! This sounds amazing. Rayla and I are coming up on our three-month anniversary. This will be the perfect way to celebrate ... in between conference speakers, that is. Thanks, man."

Dave rounded the desk and brought up the seminar schedule on Luke's Bureau laptop. "I figured you'd say yes, so I signed you up and paid your fee. Just in time, too, I'd say, as there were only a handful of spots left. The fee includes a room at Grand Hotel. Several LA White Collar agents are attending, and they're using an FBI jet to fly directly to the island, but unfortunately, there weren't any seats left. Rayla couldn't have gone with you if you'd opted for that mode of transportation, anyway. You're going to have to catch a commercial flight."

Dave went the extra step and accessed air accommodations to Michigan, finding another non-stop flight out of LAX that afternoon. "You'll probably have to hustle to catch it. I hope this is enough time for Rayla to grab extra leave from her job. I would have given you more warning, but this intel arrived with my mail from DC this morning."

"She's COO at her company. She pretty much does what she wants, but I'll give her a call right now before I book the flight."

"Your second in charge is Ian Sachs, right? He up for a few days without you so soon in his new position here?"

"More than," Luke answered.

"Great. See you on Monday."

As Dave walked out of Luke's office, Luke's eyes darted upward. "Thank you!" he whispered in prayerful reverence.

14

THOUGH SHE COULD HAVE opted to ride her chartered flight directly onto the island, Rayla decided against the more convenient option. Since she'd arrived with a couple days to spare to surveil and enact her scheme to save the diamond, she decided to land in St. Ignace and use the rest of the day to travel to the island the way she and her parents always had—via a catamaran from Mackinaw City. That plan afforded her the opportunity to drive over the Mackinac Bridge, another delight for this combination mission and trip down memory lane. She rented a car at the airport and got to it.

After paying the bridge toll at the St. Ignace booth, Rayla fixed her excited gaze on the beckoning sights of the first leg of her journey across the five-mile suspension bridge. Soon, the dark, glassy water beneath and all around her surged outward, becoming shades of light to deep blue. The swirling water vied for her undivided attention, much like a fireworks display demands its audience's appreciation. With it, a childhood memory emerged: The sound of the crystal water gently lapping against the bridge's support pillars at the waterfront park of the Lower Peninsula while she threw breadcrumbs to the seagulls. That sound had always been soothing and mesmerizing.

Now, so many years later, she didn't want to look away from the magical sight before her, the visual experience more picturesque than she recalled—likely more so because she hadn't experienced the glorious view in a while. Unfortunately, she couldn't keep her eyes locked where she desired; she had to drive, too. Dad had always driven in the past, permitting her to take in every inch of the extraordinary Straits of Mackinac.

The apex of the bridge between the two impressive spires—a height of somewhere around five-hundred-fifty feet, if memory served—allotted the most breathtaking view of the opulent waters. She quickly sucked in a lungful of air, realizing she had stopped breathing. Here she was, in the middle of the Mackinac Bridge, reliving her childhood and once again appreciating a sight she had once taken for granted. *Outstanding!*

On the southern side of the bridge, the Lower Peninsula of Michigan—or "the mitten," as she liked to call it—she drove to the Star Line Ferry dock. After tipping and handing over her keys to a valet who would drive her rental to the long-term parking lot, she enlisted the help of a ferry worker to ensure her luggage made it aboard the catamaran. Then, she bought a ticket and waited on the dock amidst a line of vacationers.

It was a beautiful mid-September day all around the Mackinac area. A few puffy white clouds dotted the horizon amidst an abundance of sunshine as far as the eye could see. The temperature was easily in the low to mid-seventies, unusually warm for this time of year in Michigan, and even more so because it was going on six p.m. in the Eastern Time Zone. She couldn't have chosen a more perfect day for her first-in-five-years' visit.

Once the catamaran arrived at the Mackinaw City dock from the island and the departing passengers cleared the ramp, Rayla queued up with the others to board. She'd ridden on the very top level of the ferry as a young girl many times. The completely open deck allotted hearty souls the Straits' hefty breezes and sometimes a little, or even a lot, of lake spray. She wouldn't be riding up top today, however. It was a tad cool for her taste. She settled in the first deck cabin next to a left-side window and looked forward to the prominently featured, picturesque view of the bridge she'd be awarded on the ride to the island.

Like everything else she'd experienced to this point in her northern Michigan visit, the eighteen-minute trip to Mackinac Island seared into her very being with a "welcome home, Rayla" kind of vibe. Although many times in the past the waters had been rough, and "the Cat" had pitched and rocked, today the lake was relatively calm. It was smooth and comfortable sailing to the place she had always described as paradise. She'd been to many wonderful places on this planet, but Mackinac Island remained her favorite.

At the island's dock, she disembarked the ferry and walked the thirty or so yards to the awaiting Grand Hotel carriage, taking in the area's sights and sounds, as well as the unique smells—a blend of horse manure and fudge. Two majestic black horses decked out in fancy black harnesses were hitched to the satiny-smooth, burgundy and black landeau.

She dipped into her purse for the baggie of carrots she'd brought for this occasion, asking the coach driver's permission before feeding the stately steeds their well-earned treat. Rayla had known beforehand, carriage drivers never allowed visitors to treat the horses. But she was fairly certain, upon seeing the carrots in her hand, this jolly-looking driver would give in ... just this once. She wasn't disappointed. He smiled congenially and dipped his head. Her heart swelled, her smile growing ever wider as the horses crunched up the snacks in obvious appreciation.

The portly coach driver—dressed in formal attire complete with top hat and white gloves—helped her board the enclosed, eight-passenger coach. Without question, Grand's carriages, which provided their guests luxury transport to the hotel, were the most ornate on the island. Only two other passengers, a delightful elderly couple, had boarded the coach before the driver mounted the rig and started them on their way. Their luggage had preceded them on another horse-drawn wagon.

Rayla thoroughly enjoyed the ride through the island's downtown area, observing the other horse-drawn carriages, bicyclists, walkers, and even the horse-poop-scooper guys with a smile she couldn't turn off. Main Street hadn't changed one iota since her last visit. Various types of restaurants and fudge, souvenir, and bicycle rental shops lined both sides of the street, packed together as one building with no space between them except the interior walls separating the shops. Occasionally, a side street ended the one-building line, which picked up again on the other side.

A quarter mile or so down Main Street, they took a right on one of those side streets then a left onto Market Street, passing by the local police station and courthouse on the right, and riding stables, bed-and-breakfast inns, and more quaint souvenir shops on the left. Another right turn onto Cadotte Avenue began the almost immediate forty-degree climb that led past the little stone church she'd always dreamed she'd be married in. Possibly another eighth of a mile on the left and opposite the church, Grand Hotel spread out in all its close to three-hundred-fifty-thousand square feet of majestic glory. She'd seen the massive structure countless times, stayed in it every summer she was growing up, but gazing at it never got old. The front porch alone, the longest in the world, spanned an impressive six-hundred-sixty feet.

When the coach stopped at the main entrance, Rayla glided out and helped the elderly couple, George and Aubrey Finnigan, navigate the step down from the carriage. Then, she accompanied them into the lowest-level—the lobby of the six-floor structure where the registration desk was located—taking a moment to admire the grass-green, black, and magenta-colored mosaic of a coach and driver weaved into the pristine carpet.

After she and the Finnigans checked in, she bid the couple a pleasant stay and climbed the gold-banistered, red and black-carpeted stairway to the next floor—the Parlor level. She hiked around the vast area, refamiliarizing herself with the many rooms and exhibition areas—the Trophy Room, the Art Gallery, the Audubon Wine Bar, and the expansive sitting area, to name a few. After scanning the busy Main Dining Room, she backed up and peeked into the Terrace Room, where a six-piece jazz band and vocalist prepared to entertain formally dressed guests with snappy music and dancing, the evening's highbrow activity.

The irrepressible smile, which had most certainly adorned her features from the moment she'd stepped off the ferry, began taking its toll. Her face hurt, but that didn't make a bit of difference. Rayla continued grinning as she mounted the stairs past the first, second, and third floors to the fourth floor. Her room, the first to the east of the cupola, though a few stairs down from the Cupola Bar's lowest level, was basically adjacent to it and the resplendent chandelier that housed The Maiden of St. Marys diamond.

Naturally, she climbed the stairs to the bar before checking out her room, snatching her first view of The Maiden in five years. As soon as her gaze landed on the stunning stone, she practically drooled. In that moment, she vowed never again to stay away so long.

She wanted to circle the area where the chandelier hung between the two floors of the Cupola Bar, to let her eyes drink in the beauty of the perfect gem housed within the extraordinary light source from every angle, but she knew better. She shouldn't call undue attention to herself as someone who had shown more than a passing interest because, if all went to plan, she intended to steal the diamond late Friday night, shortly before the other thief or thieves would do so to complete the challenge on Saturday. Although she intended to put it back, the other thief would steal her replica, thereby leaving the chandelier barren of its treasure or her forgery for at least twenty-four hours. No way did she want the police looking too closely at her during their investigation.

She snapped a few pictures with her phone, an action that would certainly go unnoticed by the employees and other tourists but would aid her in planning the heist. Then, she headed to her room. She didn't stay long, however. Seeing her luggage had been brought up and perhaps a little overexcited to resume her investigation of the massive, extravagant hotel, Rayla used the bathroom and then left to dine in the Main Dining Room without more than a cursory glance at her accommodations.

After wolfing down a superb supper, she got back to business, conducting an exhaustive tour of the hotel's interior. She practically swallowed her tongue when she saw the easel bearing the Michigan State Police seminar information at the entrance to the Grand Pavilion, the hotel's newest and largest conference room at the north end of the Main Dining Room.

The placard on the easel featured the official Michigan State Police logo with "Intricacies of the World of Forgery Seminar, Thursday, September 17 - Saturday, September 19" emblazoned underneath. For a mere heartbeat, her blood ran cold when she read the bottom line: "Welcome FBI Special Agent Charles Milford, Keynote Speaker, and all Federal and Multi-state Police Departments." *This place will be crawling with police and feds while I perpetrate this theft.*

From everything she knew about regular cops and FBI agents—or "suits," as the feds were not particularly fondly referred to in her world—they were here more for the booze and after parties than for any ancillary intel they might obtain on forgery schemes. That could pose a problem if they happened to be hanging out where her diamond hung—a likely possibility. She filed that thought in the back of her mind for the moment and continued her tour.

Her circuit ended at the bottom floor of the Cupola Bar, where she snapped some more pictures, acting like a tourist while paying specific attention to the large number of casually attired feds and cops who packed the place out. With that ominous sight, she obtained the bar's hours of operation, which turned out to be a little disconcerting.

Although the bartenders stopped serving drinks by eleven-thirty p.m. and were off duty at midnight, the area remained unlocked and open to the public twenty-four-seven. As unlikely as a patron initially popping in after midnight might be, stragglers, specifically alcohol overindulging law enforcement people, hanging around later were a given. In order to steal the real Maiden before midnight on Saturday, thus thwarting the challenge, she had to rethink her Friday night strategy. The situation being what it was, she needed to steal the diamond in the early hours of Friday morning—like maybe two or three a.m.—not just before midnight as she'd originally intended.

She'd planned to replace The Maiden with a forgery and then set herself up to watch the thief or thieves do their thing immediately afterward. *Well, that isn't an option anymore.* Those officers, detectives, and agents had to call it a night at some point, but it would be late, for sure. Because of that, her burglary would need to go down a day sooner, making the necessary reconnaissance tonight's job.

Her theft strategy entailed lifting the real diamond and replacing it with a moissanite replica she'd commissioned from her gem-forging specialist. Ezriel was a bona fide diamond cutting expert working in the legendary Diamond Quarter, or "Square Mile," in Antwerp, Belgium, but he had no problem creating masterful forgeries for his favorite thieves as a sideline. The second time Rayla had visited him, Ezriel had told her she was his number one favorite. She had no doubt he told every thief he worked with the same. Except, she couldn't deny the way his eyes lit up when he saw her coming. He was a flirt, for sure, and a good-looking one, too, but his eagerness for her likely had more to do with her generous payments for his work.

This time, a phone call was all Ezriel received, but he'd readily agreed to deliver. He'd had to work fast, but with Rayla's provision of precise dimensions and a texted picture of The Maiden, Ezriel had FedExed the diamond look-alike to her within two days. It now resided within a velvet pouch inside a wooden jewelry box surrounded by packing materials alongside the rest of her thieving equipment.

Despite many offers from the plethora of LEOs to take a seat with them, she nursed a club soda and lime on the upper floor of the Cupola Bar while leaning against the white banister which surrounded the chandelier's dramatic drop into the bottom level. There, she kept an eye on both floors, waiting to see when the last customers left.

As expected, both floors cleared out around midnight. She hung out in the bar for another half hour or so, watching for late-night sightseers who might pounce on the chance to look out of the one-hundred-eighty-degree panoramic observatory, but no one came in. Nobody so much as walked the hallway. Both floors of the bar and surrounding area were completely vacant.

With her surveillance completed, she went back to her room at twelve-forty-five. Having thoroughly cased the hotel and bar and satisfied she had worked through the problem of federal agents skulking about, she enjoyed a better look at her spectacular accommodations.

The east-end Cupola rooms and suites were the newest additions which brought Grand Hotel's total room count to three-hundred-ninety-seven. Her suite was not only stunning but up there as the most comfortable Rayla had had the pleasure to patronize in her career as a thief. It featured two bedrooms, a parlor, two separate three-step platforms—which provided fabulous views of the Straits from patio-door-size windows—and a bath with an extra-large, glass-encased shower. The room was papered with bright, cheerful blue and pink flowers above white paneling and ornate molding. All of the banisters for the platforms were of the same smooth, white wood.

The king-size bed in the first of the two-bedroom suite was canopied with just the right amount of firmness and four fluffy, feathered pillows. Absolutely glorious. Rayla stripped off her clothes and climbed under the silky sheets and down comforter. She must have fallen asleep immediately, because the next morning, she couldn't remember her head hitting the pillow.

15

LUKE IMMEDIATELY BOOKED the non-stop flight to Detroit, as well as a connecting flight to Pellston as soon as Dave left him. From there, his best option was to ride a shuttlebus across the Mackinac Bridge to the Mackinac County Airport in St. Ignace. It would be pretty late by the time he arrived in the northern Michigan town—close to midnight Eastern Time. The ferries to the island didn't run that late, so he booked a personal charter flight to the island from the mainland airport. Because of the late hour, the normally low-rate hopper cost considerably more, but it was on the FBI's dime. Besides, he needed to check into the conference by eight the next morning. Made no sense to spend the night on the mainland and possibly miss the check in time when he had a reservation at Grand Hotel on the island. The money he'd save from waiting for the regular flight the next morning would be spent staying at another hotel, anyway.

He took a few minutes to talk to his team and specifically, his second in command, putting Ian in charge until he returned. Then, he packed up and set out on the usual thirty-minute trip home. On the way, Moneypenny found a flight out of SBA, Santa Barbara Airport, that would get him to LAX in about half the time it would take to drive there, so he booked that flight, too. Seemed obvious that *Someone* was looking out for him, because he arrived at the LA airport in time to catch the two-p.m. flight to Michigan.

Having lost three hours in his excursion east, Luke finally made it to the Mackinac County Airport at twelve-twelve a.m. Thursday. A five-minute flight landed him on Mackinac Island, and a pre-arranged pickup by a horse-drawn carriage delivered him to Grand Hotel at around twelve-thirty-five. He registered and was in his room on the fourth floor in the hotel's east-end—a few steps down and across the hall from the lower floor of the Cupola Bar and its diamond-carrying chandelier—ten minutes before one a.m.

Luke couldn't believe his luck. He hadn't booked this particular room, didn't have a say in where he'd be placed, but here he was, as close to the scene of the upcoming heist as one could get. He knew Rayla would wait until well after hours to perpetrate, which wouldn't interfere with the conference Dave expected him to attend. All he had to do was wait until the Cupola Bar closed, then find an out-of-sight niche from which to watch the area. But he was sure he didn't need to worry about that tonight. Rayla would take at least one day to surveil before her heist.

Exhausted from the traveling ordeal, he stripped, set his alarm for seven-thirty, and fell into a very comfortable king-size bed.

It seemed like he'd barely closed his eyes when that damn alarm woke him. He wanted nothing more than to ignore it and pick up where he'd left off—some spectacular dream involving him, Rayla, handcuffs, a federal SUV chasing them with lights flashing and sirens blaring, and ... well ... a sexual fantasy he hadn't yet considered. Unfortunately, his dratted better judgement won out, and he rolled out of bed and headed for the shower.

On his way to the Parlor level and the Grand Pavilion to register, he continually scanned for Rayla, though he knew it was unlikely she'd be up at this ungodly hour. If she was, she'd likely be out running. *If only I knew the alias she's using.* That would make finding her a breeze. *I wonder if I'd get anywhere calling Devon and telling her I have an emergency and need Rayla's current information? Ha!* He knew all that would accomplish was Devon offering to call Rayla for him.

He'd seen his girlfriend's regular cellphone lying on the dresser along with her driver's license and credit cards when he'd gone home to pack yesterday morning. Rayla now possessed a wallet full of fake cards and a forged driver's license, and the Robin(s) and *Femme* always used burner phones with no GPS capability while on a job. He'd have to stick to his original plan: catch her in the act.

But he wouldn't stop her heist. He felt comfortable with his conclusion that Rayla wanted to protect the diamond while identifying and following the real thieves so they could be arrested for all of the international thefts. It was in his and the Bureau's best interest to let her play it out. As soon as she had the diamond and returned to wherever she was staying—somewhere in this hotel, he was sure—he'd confront her. Then, if he determined she had stolen it for herself, he'd deal with it. More likely, the two of them would watch a second robbery and tail the bad guy together. *She must have a plan in place to accomplish that.*

Luke made it to the seminar registration at eight a.m. on the dot. As soon as he'd signed in and received his packet and pin-on name tag, he joined the other agents in the Main Dining Room for breakfast. He recognized a few from White Collar in DC, guys he knew through Josh. The first leg of the seminar with the host speaker, entitled "Welcome to the World of Criminal Forgery," would begin at nine. Sounded boring as hell, especially since he'd received a superior education from the incomparable forgery virtuoso, Patti Nichol-Sanders herself, but he had little choice except to attend.

Nevertheless, his true reason for traveling to Michigan was uppermost in his mind, so he sat at the back of the room, closest seat to the double doors, hoping to sneak out at some point. Maybe, just maybe, he could catch a glimpse of his thieving girlfriend, possibly have a chat with her, before she heisted The Maiden of St. Marys.

16

WHEN SHE WOKE Thursday morning around eight-thirty, Rayla decreed the previous seven-and-a half hours had been the best night's sleep she'd had in ... maybe ever. She felt rested and alert, even before her first cup of coffee. *Unbelievable.*

She passed on the shower and dressed quickly, arriving for breakfast at nine—thirty solid minutes before the full breakfast in the Main Dining Room ended. She'd craved the full breakfast, and it didn't disappoint.

After filling her plate with eggs, bacon, sausage, French toast, fresh fruit, and a variety of homemade pastries, she found a table near the Grand Pavilion, hoping to hear a little of what was going on inside. Unfortunately, two *extra-stuffed* suits—their girth definitively not appealing—were closing the doors when she arrived. Too bad Devon, Amy, and Patti couldn't be here. The conference aimed to teach how to recognize all types of forgeries. As the forgery experts for the Robin(s), the matriarch-linked threesome certainly would have appreciated sitting in. It would have given them a good laugh, at the very least.

Her tummy full, she sat back and planned the day's events while sipping her third cup of coffee. After conducting her own reconnaissance the previous day, she knew a couple things about how and when the burglary would happen.

The challenge stated the theft must occur on September 19th, a Saturday this year as was the day of the previous two thefts for The Triple Crown. She'd determined, because of the

Cupola Bar's lingering late-night guests, the only time it was feasible for the other thief to make the strike while maintaining the challenge's rules would be in the early morning hours of Saturday.

Since she had no idea who was responsible for these thefts, or how they planned to get into the hotel or rob the display, she had to cover all bases. In her mind, staying at Grand Hotel made the most sense. *Clearly. That's how I'm doing it.* But there was always a chance the burglar was not staying here and would enter another way—like maybe through the outer portion of the cupola itself at the very top of the hotel. Seemed very *not* high-end to gain access that way, but there were many reasons a thief might choose to do things differently. There were surveillance cams everywhere inside the hotel, the Cupola Bar being no exception. Trivial in her mind to bypass them, but maybe this thief preferred scaling outside walls over disengaging surveillance cams. *No accounting for taste.*

Even if the criminal was staying in the hotel, perhaps he'd book it off the island via boat or airplane immediately after he had nabbed her moissanite fake. Rayla's plan to get him arrested for all three thefts hinged on her ability to follow him, thereby locating the other two gems and calling in the FBI. If the chase landed her in a foreign country, she'd enlist Interpol's help. Therefore, she needed both an airplane and a fast boat at her disposal.

On second thought, a jet alone makes more sense. She could follow a boat in a plane or jet, but if she opted to chase a boat with another boat and then The Triple Crown thief switched to a plane somewhere on the mainland, she'd be up a creek finding a way to continue her pursuit. If the flight was lengthy, a jet was more practical—for her as well as him. *A jet it is.* Thankfully, she'd thought ahead enough to have Ezriel implant her replica diamond with a GPS tracker, just in case she lost the thug. *Best laid plans and all that …*

She glanced at her watch as she rose to leave. Nine-forty-eight. Chartering a jet to remain on standby at the island's airstrip at midnight Saturday was her first order of business for today. *Then perhaps a run and a shower?*

Luke's first opportunity to leave the conference came at nine-fifty when the first presentation had completed. While the others broke into smaller groups, allowing them to move from station to station—six, kiosk-like areas where monitors replayed recorded, off-site lectures and demonstrations—Luke slipped out, feigning a need to use the restroom.

Once he'd been up and down the Main Dining Room, had checked out the continental breakfast for late risers in the Geranium Room, and lastly, had run up to the Cupola Bar to see if his honey might be scoping out the area for her heist, he realized the insaneness of expecting to see Rayla. His best chances were to have caught her at breakfast, but she either hadn't made it down or he missed her while enduring the first part of the seminar.

As for conducting her heisting reconnaissance, she'd want to do that when the bar officially opened at noon so as not to alert suspicion via the surveillance cams. *Honestly, though, she might not even be staying here.* As much as his gut argued against that possibility, there was no way to know where she was or what she was up to at this hour of the morning. All he could count on was the fact she'd burglarize the Cupola Bar diamond display sometime in the wee hours of either tomorrow or Saturday morning, depending on her reason for the heist. Friday, if she were attempting to rescue the gem; Saturday, if she wanted in on the challenge.

After returning to the Parlor level and conducting another hasty sweep, he slipped back into the conference room and took up with the group nearest the doors. Some dull, boring, monotoned moron was droning on about how to spot forged drivers' licenses. Luke was sure he'd receive a better education from Patti, just as he was sure one of her forged licenses would fool this guy in a heartbeat.

Jet secured for early Saturday morning, Rayla waited an hour to digest the way-bigger-than-usual breakfast before donning her running gear and heading out for a late-morning run. The perimeter of the island harbored an eight-mile-long, honest-to-goodness Michigan trunk line highway—the M-185—though horses, buggies, bicycles, and walkers were all that were allowed on this particular Michigan thoroughfare. It had always been a favorite run and race for Rayla.

At eleven a.m., the air was cool and crisp and the famous highway as spectacular as she remembered. She chose to run it counterclockwise, as she always did, putting Lake Huron in view all around to her right with a marvelous view of the bridge on the last leg of the run. The forest of trees, rising hills, and rock formations to her left—the interior of the island— also sparked a ton of memories. She'd missed the eight-mile road race the island hosted every year on the second Saturday of September. Running the same course this week was the next best thing.

She cruised around the island perimeter at a six-minute pace but finished the run in fifty minutes because she'd run the first mile slower, as a warmup. She jogged and walked what amounted to a ten-minute cooldown from the highway back to Grand, flew by the entrance to the Main Dining Room—which was filling up fast with the lunch crowd—and up the stairs from the Parlor back to the east-end Cupola suites.

Luke cleared out of the Grand Pavilion and turned into the Main Dining Room for what he had heard was a truly phenomenal lunch buffet, his reprieve from this boring seminar, when he caught a glimpse of Rayla as she crossed the sitting area from the front doors and started to jog up the Parlor stairway. It was her; he was sure. She'd been out for a run. He recognized her top line running gear, plus, nobody on the planet had legs as long, sleek, and beautiful as hers. He didn't see her face, but he did notice her dark brown ponytail, and he'd recognize that gorgeous body anywhere, even from the thirty or so yards between them.

He quickened his pace, almost jogging through the narrow passageway from the far east end of the dining hall to the main entrance, but too many people and servers blocked him. By the time he arrived at the stairway and dashed up, clearing three steps at a time, she was nowhere in sight. He called out her name and checked each level, hoping to catch another glimpse of her. Nada. She could have exited on any floor. She had too much of a head start for him to tail her. The hopefulness that had peaked at the sight of her was crushed ... just like that.

She'd take a shower before coming down for lunch, so he returned to pack his plate at the buffet. Then he parked himself near the dining room's entrance to the Parlor area. When he'd finished eating, he took a seat in a comfortably padded armchair in the sitting area, opposite the stairway and elevator, determined to stake out both until she reappeared ... seminar be damned.

Unfortunately, just before one p.m., two of the guys from his small group spotted him and dragged him back. No way he could refuse to return with them, so Luke had to hold out hope he might see Rayla at supper.

In her room, Rayla enjoyed one of her long, languorously warm showers, using the time to run through her heist plan—specifically, the quickest way to disable the surveillance cameras.

The bar itself sported three unmonitored, recording and video-only cams—one at the entrance of each floor above the "Exit" signs and one on the lower floor pointing at the bar's cash register area. She had already snapped the appropriate pictures which she'd use to block those when she infiltrated.

Having done her homework on The Maiden's display, Rayla knew two more unmonitored video cams were positioned on the diamond within the area where the chandelier hung. For those, she'd use pictures she'd found on the Internet and had doctored to the surveillance cams' precise specifications. All pics needed were set within magnetic frames to digital-display cameras, which in turn would attach in front of each surveillance camera.

Once the bar's observation cams were rendered useless, she'd move on to disable the laser security system which crisscrossed the entirety of the chandelier display area. She knew what to do. Disabling security cameras and lasers and implementing everything else she'd planned for this heist were typical of her normal thieving proclivities.

With her mental walk-through completed, she shut off the water, toweled dry, and emerged from the steamy bathroom. After blow-drying her shoulder-length hair and slathering on her favorite shea-butter lotion, she dressed in jeans and a toasty-warm, tight-ribbed, mock neck sweater for the day's cooler weather.

At precisely one p.m., she skimmed down the stairway to the Parlor. The grand luncheon buffet was still in full swing, but having had such a big breakfast, she passed on lunch. She had thirteen hours before she'd perpetrate her heist. Plenty of time to tour the island and reminisce. *And let's start with renting a horse for a couple hours.* That was the perfect way to check out the island's interior scenic slopes along with its ranches, mansions, and cottages.

She spent the day horseback riding, biking, touring the exhibits—such as Fort Mackinac, the Butterfly House, the Art Museum, and the oldest churches and other structures on the island—and walking around the shops on Main Street. After eating an early dinner in town, she kicked around the island some more, killing time until she watched the sun set over the Mackinac Bridge before returning to the hotel around eight.

"No frickin' way," Luke said, when his new friends from the seminar, Bruce and Toby out of the Minneapolis FBI field office, informed him about the seven to nine p.m. evening webinar being held in the Theater after dinner. "I thought we were done at six. Is it optional?"

"I don't know about your boss's mindset, but ours would say no to that," Bruce responded.

Although technically, he didn't have to report his every move to Dave, Luke guessed the Major Thefts ASAC would feel the same. With that conclusion, there went his last chance to find Rayla before she would most likely heist The Maiden of St. Marys.

17

THE ALARM SHE'D SET on her thief-savvy watch woke Rayla from her five-hour nap at one o'clock Friday morning. She turned on the in-room coffee brewer first thing and downed a cup of strong black coffee before wrapping her hair up and blasting her body with a cold shower. After toweling off, she moved about her room in the nude until her skin was completely dry—a helpful step which allowed her to easily slink into her custom-fitted black leather. When every inch of her was smooth as silk, she brought out her heisting attire and laid it on the bed.

She began the dressing-for-a-heist ritual by slipping on the sleek, body-hugging trousers, enjoying the incomparable sensual caress of the soft material against her bare skin. Next, she pulled on the lithe, over-the-knee boots which fit so snuggly, they may as well have been part of the leather pants. Boots on and zipped, she lastly donned the leather jacket—the one missing a ruffle from its backside, thanks to Luke. The thought of how her cagey, law-abiding boyfriend had obtained the decorative piece tugged out a smile. He still carried it in his wallet.

Fully and appropriately dressed for the evening's activities, she smoothed her hair with wet fingers, ponytailed her long mane, then twisted it into a tight bun, fastening it with a few bobby pins followed with a faux hair scrunchy at the top of her head.

As with any job, there could be no stray hairs of hers accidentally turning up at the scene, and that imperative was particularly important for this burglary. Luke's boss was already suspicious of her. If he somehow got wind of this theft and heard about a long dark human hair found on site, she'd be the first person he'd come after with a DNA swabbing kit.

The fake hair buns were just the ticket, and this one, dark brown with caramel highlights, didn't exactly match her hair color, either. If one of the scrunchy's hairs fell out, a forensic team would see it was acrylic, so long as it didn't take any of her hair with it. For that reason, and because it didn't cover everything, she enlisted an additional safeguard.

Although Rayla didn't tend to lose excessive hair, a lot of the other Robin(s) of the Hood did. Age didn't seem to matter, either. Some of the younger Robin(s) had an equal amount of trouble with loose strands as the older generations did. Not counting today's theft, it wouldn't have been an issue if a hair were found at one of their heists, since there were no profiles of them to compare with a stray hair, or any other DNA for that matter.

Nevertheless, they'd always made sure no part of them was left behind. It was not in their thieving nature to leave things like that to chance. Therefore, she and all the Robin(s) dampened their hair before putting it up, and those with the shedding problem used hairspray, as well. Rayla squirted on that extra precaution for today's heist, then she wiped down all her leather with a magnetized cloth. The last part was SOP— standard operating procedure.

Two minutes before two a.m., she snapped on her black leather gloves and clicked her fanny-pack tool belt around her waist, feeding a strap through a loop on the right side of the leather pants and allowing the bulk of the pack to rest a little lower on her left hip. Then, she nabbed up a black nylon athletic bag which carried a lifting/lowering harness, all cameras containing the photos to block the Cupola Bar's surveillance cams, a most remarkable wooden step stool that folded into a flat twelve-inch rectangle, and two collapsible speaker stands with an extra piece of custom piping.

She crept out of her room at exactly two a.m. Before she did anything else, she carefully scoped out both levels of the Cupola Bar, as well as the hallways. She saw no one.

Tapping nimbly up the stairs to the uppermost level of the bar, Rayla dropped the athletic bag outside the doorway in the hall and removed the step stool and one of the cameras inserted within a magnetic frame which she'd marked "#1." Step stool unfolded and placed strategically underneath the exit sign but still in the hall, she turned on the camera's digital display and locked it there. With one swift movement, she blocked the surveillance cam with a precisely duplicated picture of what it had been monitoring and clamped the magnetized frame onto the surveillance setup. One monitoring camera down, and the only surveillance she needed to deal with on the upper floor, she fished around in her utility belt for a small tube of a glue-like polymer. She squeezed a tiny amount into the doorjamb's lock and closed the door. No one would be entering through that doorway until she "unglued" it following her heist. After gathering her equipment, she fled down the stairway to the bar's lower level.

Remaining outside the entryway, she repeated the steps she'd taken upstairs to obfuscate the exit-sign surveillance camera there with her camera #2. In order to get past the cam pointed at the bar and cash register unseen, she dropped to her knees and crawled until she was beyond its range on the far side of the room. From there, she approached the device from beside and a little behind it. When her third picture was in place over the bar's final surveillance cam, she returned to the door and glued it closed. Then she turned her attention to the center of the room and the diamond-bearing chandelier.

Before she could disable the lasers, Rayla needed to incapacitate the two surveillance cameras within the display, specifically so they wouldn't catch her taking out the lasers and, of course, stealing the diamond. But, in order to do that, she had to see the lasers. With nary a thought, she dug into her tool belt and wrapped her fingers around her laser imaging scope. She turned on the high-tech device and pointed it at the chandelier. Every crisscrossing laser within the display, all previously invisible, lit up in bright red before her.

The surveillance cameras within were situated low and opposite of each other in the cubby hole of the chandelier area, both pointed at the diamond. That meant taking them out one at a time was not an option. The opposite cam would pick up her movements no matter which one she tackled first. She had to block them with still pictures simultaneously while avoiding the lasers. Not an easy feat by any means, but this was the kind of challenge she lived for. And knowing what she was up against, she'd planned ahead.

The two relatively flat visual surveillance devices were attached in opposite corners six feet apart. She put the laser imaging scope in her mouth, stooped to the nylon bag, and brought out the two three-leg speaker stands. After expanding the legs of one so as to affix the base to about five and a half feet and setting it on the floor, she placed the slightly narrower, six-inch-long custom pipe into the top nozzle, the area where a speaker would normally fit, and tightened the coupling. Then, she hoisted the second speaker stand, legs not yet expanded, upside down into the first by way of the narrower pipe. After tightening that coupling, she opened the second stand's legs to an equal width as that of the first's.

With her makeshift camera holder prepared, and her securely planted directly underneath the chandelier, she attached the last two pre-loaded cameras to the two opposite legs of the stand with strong magnets, adjusted the laser imaging scope in her mouth to show the lasers and, avoiding said lasers, set the stand in place, thus blocking the two surveillance cams both swiftly and simultaneously.

Hmmm, maybe I've just one-upped myself. She chuckled.

She didn't bask in her achievement long, however. Disabling the lasers was the next order of business, and she got right to it with the help of her laser analyzer and transmitter. Eyeing the laser setup, she set the instrument to receive the beams of light and reroute them to their originating junctions, thus clearing a space for her to reach the diamond display.

That accomplished, she adjusted the transmitter stand to the appropriate height and set it on the floor where the technological wonder continued to do its work keeping the lasers at bay. Lasers dealt with, she slipped her lifting/lowering harness from the bag and shot four compressed hooks one at a time like arrows with a bow through the display to clamp onto the banister above. Donning the harness in a sitting position, she pressed the button and rose to the thick glass encasement which displayed the diamond within the bottom portion of the chandelier.

Two or three minutes later, give or take, she had removed the entire bottom pane of the display glass—intact from its metal frame encasement—with a dissolving emollient, taken her prize from a dangling, clear glass pedestal, and replaced it with the moissanite replica. A little more of that awesome glue she'd used to seal the doors reset the glass pane within its frame. It appeared as if it had never been removed.

The Maiden of St. Marys snuggly tucked in a fanny-pack pouch, Rayla was back on the floor, harness detached, and reinstating all surveillance she'd bypassed. Before she returned to the lower level door, she scooted to the panoramic windows where she had noted an oddity she'd identified the moment she'd opened the lower floor's door. With a laugh, she pinched the object between her thumb and forefinger, and took it with her.

At the outer door, she used a syringe to squirt an acidic, glue-dissolving solution into the door lock. Opening the door and fleeing the lower level, she returned to the top floor, dissolved the glue from that lock, and removed the cameras she'd put in place to block the bar's upper floor surveillance cam.

She crept back to her room positively beaming with her success, but before she opened her door, she spun to admonish the man who appeared behind her.

"What took you so long?" Rayla asked, holding up the button cam she'd removed from the Cupola Bar window. "When I saw this, complete with your FBI equipment number, I wondered why you didn't meet me at the bar's door."

"Unfortunately, I couldn't locate you in this hotel. All I could do was watch the bar until you perpetrated your heist, except there was no place I could hide to accomplish that," Luke responded. "That's why I attached the button cam. I didn't want to break your concentration, so I watched your heist in high definition inside my room. Figures you'd memorize my equipment number and know I was here when you saw the button cam."

"I've known you were here since shortly after I arrived on Wednesday—well, knew you were en route, anyway. When I saw the MSP conference placard welcoming federal agents, I wanted to know if I might bump into someone, some agent who might recognize me because of you. So, I hacked Grand's computers and found the list of conference attendees. I have to admit, I was surprised to see you listed. Forgery doesn't exactly fall into the high-end theft purview." She opened her door and led them inside.

"Your heist was beyond phenomenal, by the way," he said after he'd closed the door and walked farther into her parlor. "I've longed to watch you complete a full heist. You didn't let me down in the slightest."

She dipped her head and smiled with the compliment. As she did, a knock sounded on the door.

"You expecting someone else?" he asked.

When Rayla shook her head, Luke peered through the eyehole.

His quick glance at her, coupled with the way he weaved, caused her to wonder. *Is he blanching?* Panic snaked throughout her body.

"Get to the bathroom," he instructed, "and get out of that leather."

As she whirled to obey, the door flew open, and she turned back abruptly with the man's command for her to stop. The FBI agent beyond the open door wielded a master key, and her recognition of him increased her rising trepidation.

Luke's direct superior, the new ASAC of Major Thefts in LA, wasn't smiling.

"Well, well, well," Dave said, cracking a decidedly non-jovial smirk. "Would you look what we have here. My only quandary is which one of you I should arrest first."

18

"I KNOW THIS IS GOING TO SOUND CLICHÉ, but honestly, Dave, this isn't what it looks like," Luke said, battling to keep his voice steady.

"I'll take that as my invitation to come in," Dave replied. Once inside the sitting area, he held out his hand toward Luke. "I'll listen, but not until I have your weapon and creds."

"Really? That's the way you want to play this?" Luke said incredulously.

"For now I'm going with SOP, Keltry. You need to convince me she's not a thief and you aren't complicit. If you can accomplish that, I'd be mind-blowingly impressed and more than happy to hand those back to you."

Luke acquiesced, handing Dave his gun and FBI credentials. He understood his boss's position. *And, let's face it. Rayla is a thief and I am complicit.* Even though the two of them had what he considered a reasonable explanation for tonight's theft, Rayla was unquestionably a thief. Her attire alone argued for as much. Whether Luke had known before tonight was the question Dave wanted answered first and foremost.

In any case, the fact he knew Rayla was an operating thief and not turning her in made him guilty of harboring a fugitive. He'd just seen the last of his gun and creds, but that was the least of his worries.

"How about you, Rayla? Are you packing, sweetheart?" Dave asked with a cocky grin.

Luke almost decked him for the crass, demeaning, and unnecessary way Dave had addressed her, but Rayla swiftly planted herself between him and his boss.

"No, I'm not, Special Agent Knapp. I suspect you'll be searching me. You'll find the diamond from the Cupola Bar chandelier display and a considerable cache of burglary equipment, but I have no weapons." She raised her arms for the impending grope.

Dave whisked a glance at him. Appearing to have understood Luke's anger, he became more professional, even polite. "I have to search her. You know that, right?" he said in an apologetic tone.

Luke nodded, but he cringed more at something else Dave would find: *Thief à la Femme* cards in her left pocket and Robin(s) of the Hood cards in her right. Her *Femme* identity and Robin(s) affiliation would both be laid bare. *And not a damn thing I can do about it.* Putting aside their immediate problem, Luke worried about repercussions for the rest of the Robin(s).

But when Dave had completed his search, he hadn't turned up any calling cards, and Luke understood immediately. Although Rayla was a slick sleight of hand artist and easily could have unloaded them without Dave or him noticing, it was more likely she hadn't brought calling cards for this mission. *My honey's a smart lady and thief.* They were both going to be arrested tonight, but at least she wouldn't be outed as *Femme* or a Robin(s) thief. Dave might suspect one or both, but he would have no proof. Luke breathed a silent sigh of relief, thankful for Rayla's foresight. She consistently thought of everything prior to her heists. Not planning to leave a card for this one, she'd wisely left them all at home.

Seemingly satisfied with his search, Dave agreed to sit and listen to their "dubious" explanation.

"Shall I make some coffee?" Rayla asked. While she talked, she slipped off a scrunchy of phony hair, removed a hair tie and some bobby pins, and shook out her long, dark mane, fluffing it with her fingers until the curls generated by the updo nestled seductively around her face.

Luke regarded her in awe. She didn't look riled in the slightest. In fact, she acted like an old friend had surprised them with a visit. *Well, he certainly did surprise us ...*

Dave angled his head. That gesture, coupled with his narrowed eyes and slightly agape mouth, intimated he also marveled at Rayla's cool and collected demeanor, and probably her sensual, seductive beauty, as well. "A cup of joe would be lovely," he answered, regaining his wits with a pleasant smile.

After brewing the coffee—during which time he and Dave wordlessly stared at each other—Rayla handed each of them a cup and sat next to Luke on the pink-striped sofa.

She regarded them both with a grin while taking a sip from her cup. "Who wants to start?" she asked, her expression becoming borderline mischievous.

"By all means, I think you two should," Dave said. "I'm very anxious to hear how this isn't what it looks like."

Luke met Rayla's gaze and deferred to her. He had no idea how he could get them out of this, but Rayla's con-artist charm might do the trick. She certainly was a good deal more composed than him.

"I used to be a thief," Rayla began, "a high-end thief, but apparently with too many morals for the vocation. So, I gave up the life several years ago, but I still hear things via the ineradicable thieving grapevine. When I heard The Triple Crown was going down, I was concerned about The Maiden of St. Marys. I grew up in Michigan gazing at that gem throughout my life. I couldn't bear to see it disappear, never to be seen or heard of again.

"I don't know what you know about The Triple Crown challenge, Dave, but in order to collect the promised reward from the challenge instigators, all three diamonds have to be proven stolen on precise dates. If the thief doesn't follow the challenge rules, the bounty is defunct. I just stole the last diamond needed to complete the challenge before it should have been stolen. The challenge is now officially dead, but neither the instigators nor the thief know that yet.

"You see, I replaced the real diamond with a fake, which, hopefully, will fool all of them long enough for me to find the other two gems. It is my intention, or at least it was, to watch the final theft here without leaving the real diamond in jeopardy, and then follow the thief to wherever the other two diamonds are being held. At that point, I intended to call in the FBI, or if in another country, the local feds with the help of Interpol. I want these thugs caught, and I want the other two diamonds returned to their displays in Norway and South Africa. Once I knew they'd be caught, I was going to get The Maiden into their possession so they'd face the full penalty for their thefts."

"Sounds amazingly like the type of thing *Thief à la Femme* or a Robin(s) of the Hood thief would do," Dave said.

Luke froze, but Rayla's perfectly-timed pause was calm, casual, and coupled with a smile now.

"Luke is not involved in this theft, nor did he know I was a thief in my previous life. He didn't know I was here until he showed up at the law enforcement seminar and saw me. I'm not registered under my real name, so when I realized he'd seen me, I eluded him and hid out until I perpetrated the burglary tonight. It was Luke's ill-fortune to be in the room across the hall from me. That's how he spotted me again—just now, after I perpetrated the heist. I imagine he was going to question me on all of this, but you knocked on the door before he had the chance."

Luke did everything in his power to react in appropriate agreement with everything Rayla said. She'd taught him some con-artist tricks, but he was nothing short of amazed at how easy lying was for her. *Shit, I know the truth and I believe her.* Dave, on the other hand, laughed out loud.

"That's really good, Rayla. I have to say most of it is even believable. I admire your attempt to keep Luke out of trouble, but the part about him not knowing you're a thief—used to be or otherwise—isn't true. Guess it's time you heard how I came to be here."

"I know *I'm* sitting on pins and needles to hear," Luke said with an acerbic lilt in his tone.

Dave rewarded his flare of anger with a smile. "I sent you here, Luke, specifically because I knew about this Triple Crown theft thing, and I also knew you were aware of it. From our earlier discussion, you know Josh Maddox and I have been suspicious of Rayla. You giving up your hunt for *Thief à la Femme* and the Robin(s) of the Hood just wasn't the Luke Keltry we both knew and loved. If Rayla wasn't one or both of them, then she had to be someone of equal stature to steal the obsession you had for them—pun intended."

Luke winced.

Dave continued, "When I saw the history hunt you conducted on your laptop regarding the diamond from Norway, it prompted my own research. Long story short, I believe I found everything you did, and I put it together, same as you."

"How'd you see my research?" He squinted at the man. "You hacked into my office computer?"

"You seemed off Monday evening when you left, excessively distracted. So, I let myself into your office, hoping to get some idea of what you were working on. I saw some scribbling on your desk pad about two other diamonds that had been stolen and an arrow pointing to a rough sketch of Michigan with the diamond you penciled in right about where Mackinac Island would be. My suspicions about Rayla and concern about your involvement led me to retrieve your computer activity from the FBI log. Unforgivable behavior on my part, but also unforgettable once I saw it. I needed to find out if your girlfriend was a thief, and if so, if you had any

117

knowledge of it. So, I dug around for something, anything, I could use to get you over here, or at least somewhere close by. It took me until late Tuesday, but when I found this conference right here on the island—actually *inside* Grand Hotel and within a reasonable realm of potentially useful intel for a HETU agent—I signed you up and I've been tracking your movements ever since.

"My first red flag popped when Rayla didn't come here with you as we had discussed. That wouldn't necessarily prove anything except you booked that flight for yourself alone while you were still at the office. Yet, you didn't tell me she wasn't going to attend with you. That struck me as odd. I booked a flight for the next day, and I've been sneaking around this hotel watching you. I saw you put the button cam in the bar, and I had to ask myself why you would do that if you didn't suspect she intended to steal that diamond. Couldn't come up with another answer besides the obvious. Since it's a Bureau cam, I piggybacked onto it and linked it to my computer. I watched her heist just like you did, and it was damn impressive. Add to that the fact I was right around the corner when the two of you met up outside this hotel room door, and you've got to know I overheard everything you said to each other."

"Nothing Luke and I said outside this door implicates him as having known I was once a thief who was backsliding to save a diamond." Rayla piped in. "He had his doubts about me just like you; that's why he planted the button cam. You can arrest me right now for the burglary I committed, but you have nothing to pin on Luke. He's totally innocent. For all you know, he was about to arrest me."

Luke locked eyes with his boss. "Might I suggest, instead of arresting her or me, you trust the lady is here for admirable reasons and wait out the next twenty-four hours—what I intended to do—to catch the real thief in action?"

Dave wouldn't take his eyes off Rayla, but he stood, took hold of Luke's arm, and pulled him back, though Luke doubted they were out of earshot.

"I know you think you're in love," Dave whispered, "but you've been FBI a lot longer, Luke. Why do you believe her? Seems much more likely she's feeding us both a line."

"I've known her for three months, and although you *might* be right, I could ask you the opposite question: Why wouldn't you give her a chance to prove *she's* right?"

Dave bit down on his lower lip and regarded him with a narrow-eyed grimace. Finally, his face softened. "It's like you said. I've got nothing to lose by waiting. If a second robbery goes down as she says, I'll still have to take her in, but we can talk leniency with the DA since she has no prior convictions, arrests, or warrants issued for her. If there is no second robbery—"

Luke laid his hand on Dave's shoulder to stop him from spelling out the consequences. "We agree. You've got nothing to lose by waiting."

19

"Ray? Is that you?" Devon's voice rang out through the burner phone's receiver after one ring.

"Yeah, Dev. I need to update you on what's going down over here," Rayla whispered. She was in the bathroom, supposedly using the facilities before Dave planned to transfer her and Luke to his room. Good thing she'd hidden a burner phone in every room of her luxury suite. *SOP.*

"Is everything okay?"

"Not sure yet. Let's just say things took a weird turn and I'm waiting for the outcome. There's a possibility this whole operation could go south and I'll have to run. Worst case, Luke might be coming with me. If so, we'll both need new IDs."

"What?"

A chuckle at Devon's predictable response preceded Rayla's explanation of the unexpected turn of events. Beginning with Luke tailing her, and including her successful heist of the diamond and Dave's involvement, she spelled out her plan for a possible fix. "I think this is the perfect setup for the IPA switch up. You have those creds?"

"My mom does. They're in the file cabinet where we stored them after that job."

"Good. All background updated, too?"

"I'll make sure."

"What about—"

"Everything and everybody is still in place, Ray."

Rayla breathed a little easier. "Wonderful. Can you hop a plane and get up here with the creds ASAP? Bring mine, but you should come as my superior. You dig?"

Devon laughed. "I *dig*, hon. You know I love dress up, but I think we can do better than me. I'll look into it."

Rayla knew what Devon was intimating, and if she was able to pull it off, it would be beyond fantastic. "Great! Everything needs to be ASAP, no … STAT, Okay?"

"Copy that."

"How's your job going?"

"Our group completed the mission yesterday. The Atlanta FBI picked up Mr. Brown, founder and CEO of Brown Insurance Agency on indisputable charges of fraud and racketeering. My mom, Jodi, Krista, Laura, and Katherine wrapped up the Ponzi scheme in Houston yesterday, too. Both groups flew into Santa Barbara, and we're all spending the night at my condo."

"What about Gram? I thought she was involved in one of those jobs?"

"She told us she was doing a solo thing in Europe, but I don't have any details. Didn't she tell *you*?"

Rayla hesitated, thinking. "She didn't tell me a thing. Come to think of it, she never said she was doing a job, only that she wasn't available to help me here."

"Well, you know how Evie can be. I wouldn't worry about her. On another note, I have a strange and juicy tidbit to share with you," Devon said. "Following our separate missions, when everyone arrived here, we stepped out for some celebratory drinks at the Harbor View Inn poolside bar last night, and you're never going to guess what we saw on the way over."

"Do tell!"

"We came upon a burglary going down in that swanky neighborhood down the coast from our condos. Rayla, this cute female thief with the shortest blond hair was dressed in a black tac suit, but wearing no head covering and not nearly enough black goop on her face and around her eyes to mask her. My gran and Tarry recognized her. Turns out, they and you had just met her on Monday—at Luke's office. She's the assistant resident agent of the Ventura FBI office, a certain Special Agent Deb Sines."

"Holy… Were Patti and Aunt Tarry sure?"

"Absolutely sure."

"Did you guys confront her?"

"No, we parked out of sight and watched her flawlessly rip off the snooty, better-than-thou Congressman and Mrs. Breland, cheering for her the whole time. She's good, Rayla. Really good."

"I can't believe it. Luke is surrounded by thieves, and not only us. The head honcho of the Ventura office, Special Agent Barb Sutherlin, is a reformed thief, and now we find out her second in charge is a moonlighter? I can't wait to tell Luke!"

"That explains the weird vibe I got off her when we were officially introduced in Barb's office," Luke said when Rayla relayed Devon's intel on Deb Sines.

Dave had them sequestered—okay, locked up like prisoners—in the back bedroom of his two-bedroom suite. Luke had immediately checked for listening devices and found Dave had planted two—no doubt his reason for letting them stay together. He and Rayla would definitely be providing the ASAC with information suggesting their forthrightness and complete innocence later, even though Dave had to know Luke would check for the devices. But for now, he invited Rayla to take a shower with him in what he knew to be the bug-free bathroom.

There, he turned on the fan, the shower, and the sink faucet—just-in-case precautions. Then he went ahead and undressed her. *May as well get the fun shower as long as we're in here.* Seeing Rayla naked split his attention, however, requiring him to continually refocus on the conversation for which he'd brought her in here. He wanted to talk about their problem, but she seemed unconcerned with that, telling him about Deb Sines instead while she undressed him.

"Weird vibe?" Rayla asked, as they stepped into the shower and she began soaping him up.

"She did this eye-lock thing, but not flirting. It was like she was challenging me, as if we were competing for the same job. We work in totally different departments. I couldn't understand why she'd see us as competitors. I sure as hell get it now. She's an agent herself, working next door to the FBI's High-End Theft Unit while moonlighting as a thief. 'Catch me if you can, hotshot,' is the look she gave me. I see it clear as day now."

"What are you going to do about it?" Rayla asked. She followed the question with a sensual moan as he slowly and methodically massaged her wet body with his soapy hands.

Even with his own desire rising, he paused to snap her a disbelieving gape. "There's only one way this deal with The Maiden plays out, sweetness. We're both going to jail. I'm not going to be in a position to do anything about Special Agent Sine's thieving sideline."

"That's not the way I have it worked out," she said, a smile parting her lips. "We're not going to spend one day in jail, hon."

The set of her features provided the perfect *Thief à la Femme*, "Stop worrying, I've got this under control" look. A fragment of hope he'd seen her display before, and one Luke tended to believe. She appeared especially confident now. Still, it was hard to grasp how she could possibly get them off scot free.

Nevertheless, he played along, proffering a devilish snicker. "In that case, if I'm still an agent working as the head of the west coast HETU, I'm going to catch her—with your help, of course."

"Oh, no. Really? Devon said she's very good, and she did rob a loathsome reprobate."

"I said I'd catch her, to prove I'm up for her challenge. I didn't say I'd turn her in."

"Right!" Rayla winked.

"Now, would you please tell me how you plan to get us out of this mess with Dave?"

"You know half of what I've put in play from my spiel earlier. We're attempting to catch the real thief or thieves, so it starts with staking out the Cupola Bar early tomorrow morning then following the thugs to wherever they've stashed the other two diamonds via the jet I have on retainer. What happens after we catch these guys and return the stolen diamonds depends on Dave and what he's willing to let slide. If he's okay with the story I gave him, believing you're innocent and I'm a retired thief he doesn't need to lock up, even if it means keeping a close eye on me, we'll go with that. If he's going to be a jerk about it, I'll have to implement plan B."

"Plan B? Please tell me it doesn't involve us becoming fugitives?"

"Quite the opposite, love. It involves your total exoneration, and me? Well, you won't have to worry about me at all." She scrunched her nose with a roguish grin.

He wanted to ask, but he was hopelessly sidelined with his soapy, slippery, gorgeously naked girlfriend. This could very well be the last intimate encounter they'd have together. He was damn well going to make the most of it.

20

During the Cupola Bar's regular business hours on Friday, with Dave watching her like a hawk, Rayla adhered two button cams on each level of the bar area, considerably more innocuously than Luke had done for her theft.

As Luke had determined, there honestly wasn't a way to physically stake out the bar. There was no place to hide. The button cams provided real time streamlining to the laptop she and the two FBI agents had set up in Luke's room.

Across the hall from Rayla's Cupola suite, Luke's room was closest to the bar—even closer than hers. As soon as they saw the heist completed, they could clandestinely follow the thieves immediately. Dave's room was quite a bit farther away, on the third floor and the west wing of the hotel.

So, as it turned out, Luke's room was where they were holed up at around two a.m. on Saturday morning when Rayla heard the unmistakable sound of her door closing across the hall, and a gazillion thoughts raced through her mind all at once. A lifetime of memories pieced together in a millisecond, and with them seemingly random circumstances knitted together seamlessly, finally making sense of years' worth of previously inexplicable incidents:

The trip she and Gram had taken to see The Levanger Lynx when she'd been ten, coupled with a computer view of The Contessa, her education about The Triple Crown challenge, and the stern warning Gram had given her never to steal those three diamonds—not individually or for the heisting challenge...

The first time she'd seen The Maiden of St. Marys hanging in the Cupola Bar chandelier after the trip to see The Lynx with Gram, and how the knowledge of The Triple Crown challenge had renewed her love for The Maiden and instilled a desire within her to protect the beautiful diamond at all costs...

A somewhat skirted answer to her question about how her grandfather had died, and the punishment Gram had threatened if she ever asked about his death again...

Finding out when she was twelve that her grandfather had an older brother—her granduncle—whom she had never met nor even knew existed...

Gram sending her to rescue stolen Vettes while she had gone to Cape Town to *supposedly* protect The Contessa and her fixation now on the flawlessness of that heist and the one targeting The Lynx...

A date she suddenly remembered in connection with the challenge: July 5th ... *fifty years ago*...

And finally, when her brain felt as if it might burst, one more date reverberated in her head: September 12th, sixteen years ago. That was when her grandfather had fallen from a four-story building during a heist. He'd died from internal injuries two days later. *The Cape Town Diamond Museum is four stories high*...

Rayla locked her eyes on the door, but she didn't move. Right then and there, she knew there wouldn't be a theft inside the Cupola Bar tonight. If there wasn't, Dave wouldn't believe her story, and she most certainly would go to prison as the lone thief of The Maiden of St. Marys. But she didn't care. She'd rather be locked up than let the person on the other side of the hall be caught—the person who had waited for her to steal the diamond and then planned to steal it from her. Except the diamond wasn't in her room anymore. Dave had it tucked away in his room safe.

Gram hadn't counted on that.

21

LUKE SPRANG UP and moved toward the door when he heard Rayla's suite door closing across the hall, but Rayla blocked his path. Understanding flooded in like an avalanche of smothering snow. There were a list of people Rayla would fight to protect—any one of the sisterhood among them. But no, he couldn't, wouldn't, let her take the fall for anyone, though clearly, she intended to. She fought him, but not the way she'd fought him the first time they'd tangled—the first time he'd laid eyes on her during her heist in Virginia. Her effort now was weak, as though she didn't have the energy to take him on. Instead of her slick Krav Maga moves, she held his wrists and beseeched him with puppy-dog eyes. She was hopelessly confused and ... devastated. Whoever Rayla had fingered for this, the concept of that person as the thief had so appalled her, she couldn't move.

With little effort, he pushed her aside, opened the door, and panned the hallway until he saw a figure—decidedly female—escaping down the hallway to the right. Snatching another glance at Rayla with Dave looking on, he took off and gave chase.

He contemplated the situation as he went. Whoever she was, it didn't make sense for her to run. She didn't have the diamond, nor could she be conclusively accused of having broken into Rayla's room. There had been no heist executed in the Cupola Bar, either. She had nothing on her that would incriminate her. As far as he could tell, she wasn't even wearing thieving gear. The female who either had been trying to break into or had successfully broken into Rayla's suite was dressed in regular clothes. She didn't look like a thief in the slightest.

Why is she running? Even if she's one of the Robin(s), all she has to do is pretend to be staying here and out for a late-night ice run or something. She's got to know Rayla and I will say we don't know her. Dave couldn't possibly finger the lady as a Robin(s) thief. All he'd have was some random woman being out and about at a very strange hour of the morning. He couldn't arrest anyone for that. But a little more thought put the situation in a possibly different light.

Dave strongly believed Rayla was one of the Robin(s) of the Hood and knew they were matriarchal. If he saw another female, especially at this hour of the morning, he'd connect the dots. Although a confrontation with that person wouldn't get him a name or any substantiated evidence she was connected to Rayla or the sisterhood of thieves in any way, Dave would get a picture and have another face to add to his list of suspects. As Luke had observed earlier, every breadcrumb was a step closer to the Robin(s)' undoing. *I can't let that happen.*

He whirled around. Dave had not cleared the doorway before the suspect was out of sight, skimming down the stairs, and he was still a ways behind. Luke was sure Dave didn't know who or what he had been pursuing. He slowed his pace for the few more feet to the stairway banister.

There, he flung his head over and saw Evie on the last Parlor floor landing. She glanced up, and he stared back, completely debilitated by his dumbfounding discovery. When she smiled up at him and popped a thumbs up, he hung an arm over the banister, robotically returning the gesture. She then fled down the final set of stairs to the Parlor. She was completely out of sight when Dave arrived at Luke's position.

"What the hell, Luke? Who were you chasing, and why did you stop?" Dave asked.

Luke regained his composure with commendable speed. "I think a ghost," he replied. "It's crazy, really. I heard something in the hallway, but all I saw was what looked like a blur, and it disappeared before reaching these stairs."

"Let's have a look downstairs," Dave said.

As they descended, his head reeling from having seen Evie, Luke posited the all too true theory that the real thief knew Rayla had stolen the gem and had tried to steal it from her. "Probably didn't know about you confiscating it," Luke said.

"You think what you heard was someone breaking into Rayla's room?" Dave asked.

"More likely coming out after having searched for the diamond and not finding it. Otherwise, I would have caught him."

"Plausible," Dave responded.

When they reached the Parlor level, they split to look for suspicious characters, which would have been anyone at all at two in the morning. During that time, Luke remembered Rayla's burner phone, the one she'd kept with her when she'd talked to Devon in the bathroom. He was so grateful she'd given him the number. He ducked into the Trophy room and texted her: *Jimmy your lock. Scratch it so it's noticcably been picked. Evie's disappeared. She's safe, and a scratched lock should put you in the clear.*

Minutes later, Dave met up with him at the bottom of the staircase. "Let's have a look at Rayla's door. Chances are, if someone broke in, there'll be telltale signs," he said.

Rayla was coming toward them from the other end of the hallway when they arrived at her suite. "I think I must've heard what you heard, Luke, so I went in pursuit in the other direction, just in case. Sounded like my door was locking shut. Is that what you heard?"

Luke nodded, desperately fighting the urge to snicker when he saw the mangled lock. He let his boss believe he'd seen it first.

"Geez," Dave said. "This lock has definitely been picked, and very shoddily at that. Not particularly high-end, are they?"

Rayla peered over Luke's shoulder at the lock. "That's likely why they wanted me to do all the work."

Dave jiggled the handle. Despite the scratches and dents in the deadbolt, the door remained locked. The agent dug around in his pocket and brought out three hotel keys—his and the two he'd confiscated from Luke and Rayla.

With the door open and the room visible, what they saw shocked Luke. Furniture was knocked over, pictures were off the walls or hanging crooked, and every bed had been uncovered. The mattresses were half off the beds or lying on the floor. A full sweep of the two-room suite revealed nothing had gone unturned. The place was trashed. How had Rayla managed to do all of this and still gotten down the hallway to appear she was coming back from her own search? His attention snapped to Dave, who had picked up the in-room phone.

"This is Special Agent Dave Knapp. There's been an incident. I need to talk to the manager immediately."

During the minute or so wait that ensued, Luke sought Rayla's gaze, but hers was focused on some unidentified point straight ahead of her. When they finally connected, her eyes belied her usual calm. *The tossed room is a good thing for her, isn't it? What has her rattled?*

Momentarily, Dave was speaking to the manager, asking her to meet him in his room on the third floor. "And bring a couple security officers with you," he added.

The walk to his superior's room seemed interminable, as Dave walked behind them and Luke attempted to read Rayla's emotions through her stiff posture to no avail.

Security awaited them at the hotel-room door. When the manager arrived, Dave laid out the events of the past twenty-four hours. He ended his spiel with, "I locked the diamond in my hotel safe. I'd like to hand it off to you and your security team now."

Despite what he'd said, the man cast a narrowed gaze at Rayla.

That's when Luke got it. Dave had left Rayla alone when he took off after him to pursue what was supposed to be the real thief. Now, the agent clearly had some doubt about Rayla's claim she'd been out looking, too, when she'd left the room after them. His next action confirmed Luke's suspicion.

Taking hold of Rayla's arm, the Major Thefts ASAC unlocked his door. Once inside, he pushed Rayla in front of him, and with a hand on her back, went directly to the safe. There, he turned to a security officer and said, "Keep her secured."

The officer nodded and took hold of Rayla's arm, while Luke ogled his boss. But everything fell into place when they opened the safe and looked inside. Empty. A thorough search of the room also yielded nothing.

The diamond was gone.

Luke's heart sank. Without taking another minute to contemplate other possible explanations for the theft, Dave stepped to Rayla and swung her around. This time, he didn't ask permission before searching her. Finding no diamond, he nevertheless secured her hands behind her and cuffed her while reading her her rights. "Rayla Rousseau, you are under arrest for the theft of The Maiden of St. Marys diamond. You have the right to remain silent. If you give up that right, anything you say can and will be used against you in a court of law. You have the right to an attorney. If you cannot afford an attorney, one will be provided for you. Do you understand these rights as I have explained them to you?"

"I do," Rayla replied, while Luke cast the love of his life a pained expression.

"Dave—" Luke prepared to launch into his protest, but the man cut him off abruptly.

"Not a word, Keltry. You should be glad I'm not arresting you, too."

22

RAYLA TRIED HER darndest not to smile while Dave rattled off her rights and then the "requirements" Grand's general manager needed to procure for him as they descended to the Parlor from the west-wing of the third floor. His main request was the notification of the island police. Dave wanted her locked up in a proper cell for the night. "Please tell me they have jail cells at the police station?" Dave asked, his air of superiority, slight though it was, not hard to miss.

The manager took his attitude in stride, responding with a wisp of humor-laden sarcasm. "Interrogation room, too, should you require one, with a *fancy* two-way mirror."

Dave caught on and offered an apologetic grin. "Thank you, ma'am. I appreciate your help in this matter, but I'm going to interrogate her here while I wait for the police to arrive. Anyplace in particular you'd like me to handle that?"

"The Art Gallery is right over here," the manager suggested as she stepped in that direction. "We use it for conference registrations, and a table and several chairs are still set up."

Dave pushed Rayla in front of him and followed after. Fortunately, no late check-ins or night owls were about. "Looks fine," he said. Seated in the room with Luke next to him and Rayla across the table, the ASAC began questioning her.

"Where'd you stash the diamond, Ms. Rousseau, or whatever your name really is?"

"I don't have the diamond, Special Agent Knapp. You took it from me, remember?"

"Don't pretend you don't know what I'm suggesting. When Luke and I took off on that wild goose chase, you picked the lock, trashed your room, then ran down to mine, picked in, and stole the diamond out of the hotel safe. It will go easier for you if you just admit it."

"Are you listening to yourself? That's crazy! I truly appreciate your opinion of my expertise, but no one could have accomplished all of that in the short amount of time you were gone. Besides, even if I were trying, I couldn't have messed up a lock as bad as *someone* did mine." She glanced at Luke who was unsuccessfully trying not to snicker.

As Dave opened his mouth to contest her denial, they were interrupted by three individuals who had entered through Grand's front doors—one of whom was the island's chief of police.

"Hold up there," the chief said as he entered the Art Gallery-turned-interrogation room. "We have a situation that requires some discussion."

Rayla wheeled around to see the chief, another island police officer, and a smartly dressed, dark-skinned woman heralding short brown and red-highlighted hair. The tall, thin, and stunning woman, who looked to be in her mid-to-late thirties, happened to be a former Robin(s) client, and one Rayla knew well. *Devon pulled it off. Fabulous!*

The chief introduced himself to Dave and Luke as the two FBI agents stood, apparently assuming Luke was in on the arrest—though Dave had not returned Luke's weapon or creds to him. After Dave reciprocated with his and Luke's names and titles, the chief introduced the woman.

"Agent Knapp and Keltry, this is Police Lieutenant Deidre Saber from Washington, DC. She's a U.S. domestic officer for the International Police Alliance. She's here to take custody of her undercover detective, the young lady you have apparently wrongfully arrested."

Rayla snuck a peak just in time to see Dave visibly blanch.

"IPA? You have an investigation in process for…" Dave cut out, and Rayla guessed he was waiting for Deidre to fill in the blanks to his satisfaction.

"The Triple Crown burglaries, Agent Knapp," Deidre responded. "You have seriously thwarted our attempt to track these thieves." She dispelled a cavernous breath in believable frustration, before searing Dave with an angry gaze that settled on him like a laser dot from a high-powered weapon. "I would very much like to have my detective released." Deidre stepped forward to face Rayla. "Perhaps we can put our heads together and pick up the thieves' trail."

Dave's head wobbled. He appeared frustrated, confused, and seriously pissed all at once. "I'm going to need some identification, *Lieutenant*," he said between gritted teeth.

"Of course," Deidre answered. She slipped out two ID billfolds, hers and Rayla's, and opened them. Both carried the official impress-stamped IPA insignia on thick plastic credentials and authentic International Police Alliance badges.

Rayla beamed with delight. Of course the creds were flawless, but the best part was that the ID listed her real name as Police Detective Sergeant Rayla L. Rousseau in the international organization. She would be able to sustain this facade indefinitely, getting Dave off her case so she could maintain her thieving careers, her cover career at ARI, and her relationship with Luke. *Perfect.*

Dave perused the two billfolds, going so far as to remove the cards from behind their see-through plastic sleeves in order to scrutinize them more closely. After analyzing the impressed insignia and the raised letters unique to the IPA organization, he ran a thumb and finger over the glossy surfaces, no doubt checking for yet undried ink. He then tested the resiliency of the credit-card-thick IDs.

"These look legit," he finally said, but I'd like to have one of the FBI's foremost forgery experts, who happens to be on site, examine them."

"Not a problem, Agent Knapp," Deidre replied. You can also call IPA's main office in Washington and check our backgrounds with the U.S. domestic office. Police Detective Sergeant Rousseau and I are both listed as officers in good standing. My direct superior is Captain Jonathan Durand. I'd give you the number, but I'm sure you're going to want to come by that on your own. You strike me as being as suspicious as you are thorough."

At that point, while Dave instructed the manager to locate and awaken the FBI agent who was the keynote speaker for the forgery seminar and get him to come down, Rayla snatched a glance at Luke. It was hard to define his expression. *Shock definitely works.*

"In the meantime, would you please be so kind as to release my detective," Deidre said. "We'll all wait right here until you're satisfied. You have my word, as well as the island's chief of police and his officer for back up."

With lingering annoyance, Dave stepped toward Rayla to comply with the IPA lieutenant's request, but Rayla gave in to her unrestrainable urge to stick it to Dave. She stood, and before the ASAC had swung her around, she picked out of the cuffs and handed them to him.

Dave's slitted eyes shot daggers at her. "She's a thief," he said, whirling to face Deidre, "and a damn good one. I watched her flawlessly steal the diamond from its display in the upstairs bar. You hire thieves in your organization, Lieutenant?"

"We train officers in various disciplines. You're right. Rayla is an accomplished thief, but only for the IPA."

"You sure about that?" Dave snipped.

Deidre merely smiled. "Pretty sure, Special Agent Knapp. Granted, we can't always keep an eye on our officers, but they don't get a lot of time off. I'd be surprised to find out PDS

Rousseau had perpetrated any illegal burglaries. She's been a model officer from her first day on the job."

"And when would that have been, Lt. Saber?"

"Mmm, let's see. She graduated from Michigan State University in May and has been with us in various cities throughout the U.S. until she was recently stationed out of our LA office. She's currently residing and working in a small satellite office in the Santa Barbara area. I believe you moved there in June, wasn't it, Rayla?"

"I flew into Santa Barbara on June 11th after spending a few days at the LA office."

"So, when was she trained as a thief?" Dave pressed.

Deidre answered without hesitation. "That element of her training was ongoing throughout her four years in college. Rayla signed up with us during her senior year of high school. We're a lot like the military that way. Once you sign up, you go through the equivalent of ROTC while in college—except the training is police-specific. In Rayla's case, she showed a remarkable talent for theft-related techniques, so she primarily pursued burglary training."

"Primarily?" Dave questioned.

"She was trained in all aspects of police work. She's also one hell of a shot with both rifle and handgun."

Dave's eyes never let up from their narrowed, disbelieving squint, even as he turned them on Rayla. "Why didn't you tell me any of this? Why'd you let me arrest you without announcing yourself as a law enforcement officer?"

"I can answer that, Special Agent Knapp," Deidre said. "Detective Sergeant Rousseau is under orders to maintain her undercover status at all costs, and she had no credentials with her here that would have backed such a claim. If I hadn't arrived, she would have used her phone call to contact the office. At that time, you would have been looped in."

"Why are you arriving now, Lt. Saber, and with the island police escort? It's two in the morning."

"We knew the theft would take place in the early hours of this morning, Agent Knapp. I was supposed to be here Friday evening, but things went awry at the home office. I got here as soon as I could. Knowing the theft had likely already happened, or was in progress, I brought the Mackinac Island police with me in case Rayla needed back up."

Dave's narrowed gaze softened a tad. "I'd like that number you have for IPA in DC, Lieutenant. I want to compare it to what I find in my own search for your organization. Also, I'd like the west-coast number."

"Certainly, Agent Knapp," Deidre answered with a curt head dip. She slipped a hand into her pocket and retrieved two business cards, which she handed him. "Both numbers will get you IPA switchboards, where the police detectives on duty will be able to answer your questions via a computer lookup, even if you want to call now. Since it's Saturday, not to mention the ungodly hour, you won't be able to get a hold of Captain Durand through the DC IPA office." She took out another card and scribbled some numbers on the back. "Here's his cellphone number, and I added mine, as well. If you call his cellphone, I'd recommend waiting until at least nine."

"Of course," Dave replied. Returning to his suspicious gaze, he asked, "Why did IPA send an undercover detective to Michigan all the way from California? I assume you have other officers trained in the burglary unit who would have been closer."

"As I said, Rayla exhibited an outstanding talent for burglary. She likely would have been our first choice in any case, but because she is also from Michigan and it was determined she knew the island and hotel well, she became our trained thief of choice for the covert assignment."

At that moment, the manager descended the main staircase with Special Agent Charles Milford, the leading forgery expert for the entire intelligence community—in his pajamas and robe. Dave converged on the man, presenting the IPA creds to the nation's most coveted forgery expert.

"I'm sorry to drag you out of bed, Special Agent Milford, but I need your expertise. I'm ASAC Dave Knapp from Major Thefts in LA. I'm here pursuing a diamond theft that has occurred in this hotel. This woman claims to be a Lt. Deidre Saber from the International Police Alliance. I need confirmation these creds are legitimate, sir, for her and her undercover detective."

Milford, a man in his fifties, took the creds from Dave, asked for a glass of water, and slid his glasses and a loupe from his robe pocket while he shuffled to the chair next to the one Rayla had vacated. Seated, with the creds removed from their billfolds and laid out before him and the water delivered, he began his examination.

Rayla snatched another glance at Luke. She was sure he was holding his breath.

23

THE INTERNATIONAL POLICE ALLIANCE. *Incredible.* Luke knew about the legitimate organization. Though not affiliated, it was generally treated as an extension of Interpol, one many countries had adopted because, when all was said and done, Interpol only offered information services. To have an internationally connected police force with officers on staff in participating countries provided real-time, on-the-spot law enforcement to handle "country-hopping" criminals. The military had something similar for combat and war-related incidents with the ICMA—International Covert Military Alliance.

Still, the Robin(s)—or more specifically, Patti—had outdone themselves creating credentials for the IPA. But would the creds hold up under Agent Milford's trained eye? *And who is this woman?* Luke held his breath.

Analyzing the credentials through the loupe was followed by the water test—where the agent dipped his finger in the water and smeared it over each of the inked portions of the IDs. A minute or two tops, and Milford lowered the loupe and removed his glasses. "These are authentic, Special Agent Knapp. Both the lieutenant and her detective sergeant are legitimate police detectives of the IPA."

Luke was sure Dave noted his stunned expression, but his response wouldn't hurt Rayla or the woman claiming to be her superior. The Major Thefts ASAC would get around to asking him if he knew about Rayla's "true" identity eventually.

Without hesitation or deceit, he could and would claim he did not. As a matter of fact, he suddenly wondered if all of this *was* the truth. His head wobbled with confusion.

Dave again scanned his watch, then handed back the credentials to Lt. Saber while addressing her. "It's almost three in the morning here and in DC. I'm *requesting* you to stay in this hotel as a courtesy to the FBI, under my watch, until I finish my inquiry on your legitimacy through an FBI search and with IPA in Washington. I suspect it's not too much of an inconvenience for you to finish your night here because of the hour, anyway. I'll contact IPA later this morning. If you both check out, you can be on your way."

"I can live with that," Saber said.

"Lt. Saber," Rayla spoke up, "after we're cleared, I should retrieve the fake diamond I put in the chandelier display. We need it back."

"Oh, yes. I forgot to mention that, Agent Knapp."

Dave nodded, then turned to the manager. "These two ladies will be staying with me in *that* one's" he flicked his head at Rayla, "two-room Cupola suite." With the manager's nod, Dave lobbed his focus to Milford. "Can you get me two agents from the seminar to guard the outer doorway through the rest of the night, sir?" He swept his amused countenance back to Saber. "SOP, Lieutenant. I'm sure you understand."

Saber smiled.

"I believe I can do that," Milford answered. "But, I'm not sure I understand. Their credentials are completely authentic."

"Criminals have been known to get their hands on legitimate creds. I'm obligated to follow up with my inquiry to IPA before releasing them."

"Ah, yes. Very well," Milford responded. "I'll send two agents to…?"

Dave looked to Rayla and she rattled off her room number.

"That's in the East-Wing, sir," Dave added.

With Deidre's thanks to the island's chief of police and his officer, Dave chimed in his appreciation, as well. As the chief and his officer left, Dave escorted the four of them to Rayla's room, opened the door, and saw the ladies inside. "Take the back room so I don't disturb you when I come in. Sorry, but you're going to have to put it back together." Closing the door, the ASAC finally turned his attention to Luke.

"Did you—"

"Know anything about Rayla being an IPA police detective? No. Am I surprised? Totally. But it does explain some things, doesn't it?"

"You suspected something wasn't right with her, same as I. That's why you tried to find her when you arrived here and planted the button cam."

Luke's head dropped to his chest as he let loose a heavy sigh. "I did have suspicions about her, and you noted the same things I did. She possesses personality characteristics that scream 'secret agent' ... or, yes, 'thief.' Turns out we were right about her, and on both counts. She's a covert-trained detective who specializes in burglary, and apparently, she either wasn't allowed to tell me, or didn't feel our relationship had bloomed enough to allow me in."

He honestly didn't know what was true. Was she *Thief à la Femme* and a member of the Robin(s) of the Hood, or was she an IPA detective? Maybe he'd been duped, too. So many questions. *Damn. I wish I could talk to her alone.*

When Luke lifted his head, Dave was holding out his creds and weapon. "I'm sorry I doubted you, Luke. You, above all agents I've known, have been the most dedicated and trustworthy. I should have trusted you."

"It's all right. I totally get it," he said, taking back his FBI gear. "If I had been in your position, I would have done the same. It all looked so bad, so crazy." He eyed his boss. "You believe your call tomorrow morning will confirm their story?"

147

"No reason not to at this point. But, I'm still going to keep a guard on them and make the call."

Luke waved his hand at Rayla's door. "You want me in there with you for the rest of tonight, you know, just in case they try to make a run for it?" The offer was not as generous as it sounded. If Rayla and this other chick were planning to bolt, he'd more likely help them get away.

At that moment, two suited FBI agents arrived, complete with harnessed weapons but looking a little groggy. Introductions completed and Dave's instructions imparted to the two coffee-wielding men, Dave looked back to Luke.

"I think we're good in here. Your room's right there," he pointed. "I'll holler if we need you. Get whatever sleep you can for the remainder of the night. I'll come for you around nine. I'd like to talk to IPA's captain, not the detective on duty— although I'll go through the switchboard first. I'm sure you'll want to be with me when I make the calls."

"I do. Thanks." His suspicion reaching a peak, he eyed his boss. "You never attended an FBI forgery seminar, did you? You contrived that story to get me up here because of your suspicions about Rayla."

Dave cast him a sheepish grin, and as Luke turned toward his room, the man palmed his shoulder. "One more question? Is this going to affect your relationship with Rayla? I mean, the lying and all…"

He twisted his neck to snatch a glimpse at his boss. "I have no idea."

24

DEIDRE OFFERED UP a few shocked expletives the moment Dave had opened the Cupola suite door, and she and Rayla threaded their way through the trashed hotel suite and found the back bedroom also in shambles.

With a finger to her lips, Rayla checked the entire suite for listening devices and button cams. Assured the place was bug-free, Rayla threw all restraint to the wind and tightly hugged the Robin(s)'-client-turned-friend.

"I don't know how I'll ever be able to thank you for coming up here personally. You were exactly what I needed to reach believability status. What could be better than a real, honest-to-goodness IPA lieutenant bearing authentic credentials?"

"I appreciate your appreciation, hon, but you've got to know, when Devon reached out, I wouldn't have denied her or any of the Robin(s) *anything*. She overnighted the credentials Patti created for you, and I was on the first flight out of DC to get here. I'm just sorry I couldn't have made it sooner."

"I gather she filled you in on what was happening? You knew everything, even my graduation from MSU and current status in Santa Barbara, almost as if you'd been in on it from the get-go."

Deidre chuckled. "Devon did a great job bringing me up to speed on all of your comings and goings over the last year when she called, including your FBI boyfriend and his acceptance into the Robin(s)' inner circle. She also provided the intel on what

149

you'd told her about these Triple Crown thefts and the twist in your plan when your boyfriend and his boss showed up. She made it easy.

"Honestly, the hardest part was having to wake up the chief of police here on the island. He was kind of grumpy, but I wanted this one to go down by the book. If I hadn't given him a heads up before crashing in, he might have filed a complaint with my boss and called us all back. Nobody would've wanted that."

Rayla snickered. "They don't get this level of crime over here and getting a call from IPA probably rocked his socks off." After a laugh, she asked, "Was all of that true about training your detectives in various criminal enterprises? Like, do you really have detectives who are trained burglars?"

"Absolutely true. That was another reason this proved so easy."

"I'm glad it's factual, because I have no doubt Special Agent Dave Knapp will be looking into that aspect of IPA thoroughly." She moved the conversation along by asking how Howie, Deidre's husband, and their two seven-year-old twin boys were doing.

"Everyone's doing great, Rayla, thanks to you and the rest of the Robin(s) of the Hood," Deidre answered, tearing up. "Our family is eternally in your debt. I'll never turn down a request from you if I can help you in any way."

The Robin(s) had successfully caught the man who had stolen and fled the country with millions of dollars from the bank where Howie was General Manager—having pinned the crime on Howie. It had been one of their more interesting cases, the Robin(s) being divided as to whether they should take it on, with a fifty-fifty split. After all, Deidre was a police lieutenant, and the plea for help, sent via the dark web, could have been a set up. But, Rayla, Aunt Tarry, and the other five youngest generation Robin(s) had considered it a challenge, not a trap, and their gut instinct had been right.

After determining the claim's veracity, they'd formulated a plan to help the desperate IPA lieutenant and her innocent husband. Needless to say, when the Robin(s) had delivered justice for the Sabers, Deidre and Howie had become lifelong fans and friends.

The portion of the money the sisterhood normally would have taken for their fee belonged to the bank, not the bad guy. They couldn't keep any of it and still free Howie. Therefore, they asked Deidre to recompense their service with materials—IPA plastic cards pre-stamped with the organization logo, the specific inks, and badges—for Patti, Amy, and Devon to forge authentic IPA credentials for every one of the Robin(s) of the Hood.

Deidre hadn't batted an eye to accommodate them. IPA had let her down big time seeking justice for Howie. If not for the Robin(s), her husband would still be in jail serving out a thirty-year prison sentence. Genuine IPA credentials for the Robin(s) to use in seeking justice for others seemed more than reasonable reparation to her.

After straightening the room, Deidre sat on the edge of a bed. "You know a heck of a lot more about this case than I do. What can you tell me?"

"It's all connected to The Triple Crown challenge," Rayla answered.

"IPA knows nothing about The Triple Crown challenge or the individual thefts of The Levanger Lynx and The Contessa of Kimberley. Neither Norway nor South Africa reached out for our help. Devon said you successfully stole The Maiden of St. Marys here to protect it, but Special Agent Knapp caught you and took it from you. Knowing your excellence as a thief, it's hard to imagine how that could have happened."

Rayla sat across from her on the other bed. "It's a little more complicated. Suffice it to say, Luke following me up here raised his boss's radar. Once Luke's boss was in the mix without my or Luke's knowledge, the roadblocks became insurmountable. Agent Knapp's arrival caught me off guard, and I couldn't scramble fast enough to explain what he'd seen.

"In so many ways, though, this is the best possible outcome. You providing me with ironclad proof I'm a detective for IPA will totally appease Knapp, and finally get him off my case for good." She angled her head. "That is, if the call he makes tomorrow confirms me as legit?"

"It will. I checked in with my captain before I left, filling him in on The Triple Crown of Jewel Theft. I requested to get involved here in Michigan with one of our detectives out of LA. Meanwhile, Devon hacked IPA's system and added you to our roster there. When Knapp calls, Nara, our switchboard operator, will patch him through to the detective on duty, who will validate me personally if asked. That detective will also be able to bring you up in the system. If the tenacious special agent goes through my boss, Captain Durand will most certainly route Knapp back through the detective on duty, requesting they send the FBI our LA files. You're covered, Rayla. Devon made sure of it. I know she succeeded because I followed up."

"Good to hear."

"So, what happened to the real diamond?" Deidre asked.

"Knapp took it from me and put it in his hotel room safe. The thief stole it from him, probably before making it look like she thought it was in my room."

"Before? Why do you say that?"

"There wasn't enough time for her to ransack my room, make the necessary noise to get us chasing her, and then double back to Knapp's room. Our cagey thief must have had the diamond when she came up here."

"Her?"

"I'm not at liberty to give you much detail, but I believe I know who the thief is."

"I take it you also know why she ransacked your room when she not only knew the diamond wasn't here, but already had it?"

"She did it to put me in the clear with Agent Knapp."

"Hmm. So she's a friend. Since you know who it is, can you track her?"

Rayla's chin lowered with her angst. "Yes, Deidre, I most certainly can."

25

Luke heard Dave beating on his door at eight-fifty-five a.m. By nine, with him listening in, Dave had contacted the International Police Alliance headquarters in Washington, DC, and the switchboard operator had, out of courtesy to the FBI, patched him directly through to Captain Jonathan Durand via the captain's cellphone. A short conversation validated Lt. Deidre Saber's role—who Durand knew personally and worked with daily. Although the captain didn't know a Detective Sergeant Rayla Rousseau, he brought up the LA office roster on his computer right then and there and confirmed Rayla's position within the west coast IPA.

Dave finally gave up his witch hunt and cut them free. Interestingly, he didn't apologize for screwing up their op or detaining them. But then, nothing between any police force and the FBI should have led Luke to believe they would ever feel compelled to offer each other help or explanations.

In the hallway after releasing Saber and Rayla, Dave gave Luke his personal itinerary for the remainder of the weekend. "I'm catching the first flight out of here for home. You're welcome to join me or you can do whatever you like. I'll see you Monday morning."

"I'm staying," Luke replied. "I need to talk to Rayla. Maybe I can't get better answers while her superior is here, but she and I need to figure this out."

Dave slapped him on the back. "Good luck." As he started down the hallway, he turned back. "Can you save me a trip and pick up those button cams we left in the bar?"

"Not a problem."

Rayla, Luke, and Deidre trekked down to the Main Dining Room, arriving a minute or so after breakfast ended, but the staff graciously allowed them to fill their plates and coffee cups. Maybe their creds, complete with badges so prominently displayed had something to do with it, but Rayla didn't think so. Everyone at Grand Hotel had always been top-notch friendly and accommodating.

As soon as they were seated, Luke blasted out his questions. Rayla had to admit, though she expected her boyfriend's inquiries for the specifics, she was floored with his admission he didn't know which of her stories was accurate. He came right out and asked her if she was a Robin(s) thief or truly a detective for IPA. Swallowing down her urge to giggle, she told him everything. She was beyond relieved he didn't mention *Thief à la Femme*, because Deidre didn't know about that extended aspect to her thieving persona. In hindsight, she realized she needn't have concerned herself. Luke was always careful about keeping her two identities secret. Not mentioning *Thief à la Femme* to outsiders had become SOP for him, too.

When Rayla finished filling him in, Deidre locked her gaze into Luke's. "I'm going to assume we're good to keep each other's secret, Luke?" she asked, a smile splitting her pursed lips.

"I won't tell if you won't," he replied.

"Good. Now, I must leave you. I booked a ten-thirty flight off the island." When she stood, so did Luke, and then Rayla rose to give her a hug.

"Thanks, again, Deidre."

"You are so very welcome, Rayla. Besides, it was actually fun!"

Deidre's departure left Rayla alone with her still slightly exasperated boyfriend. As expected, the lingering questions fired from his lips like rounds from a 9mm handgun, but she had a few questions of her own.

"You saw my gram escaping, but Dave didn't?"

"That's right. She escaped from the Parlor level landing before Dave arrived at the banister. I covered for her then sent you that text as soon as Dave and I parted to search. Rayla, do you have any idea why Evie would do such a deplorable thing? This seems to go against everything the Robin(s) stand for."

"I have an inkling, but I don't want to speculate until I talk to her. You can go with me when I meet with her."

"Which will be...?"

"As soon as I can track her down. Since I'm not completely sure I'm right about her motives, I have no idea how long that will be ... if ever." The thought of never seeing Gram again left a lump in her throat.

Luke shot out his next question. "It's hard for me to know what was truthful and what was conjured, especially once Deidre got here, but when Dave first started interrogating you, you said you couldn't have jimmied open your door, trashed your room, and still lifted the diamond from his room in the time we were gone. Is that true? It wasn't you who stole the diamond back from Dave then broke into your room and trashed it. It was all Evie?"

"That's correct. I suspected Gram the moment I heard the door closing across the hall, but I didn't know for sure until you saw her and sent me the text. I saw the scratched lock," she stopped to chuckle, "a little overkill though it was, and realized she was providing me with something to deflect Dave's suspicion of me. I took off down the hall, and I really was coming up from the other staircase after trying to locate her. But I never saw her."

Luke rounded the table and sat next to her, engulfing her in a loving hug. "You suspected her immediately? Why Evie of all people?"

"I have my reasons, but as I said, I don't want to speculate. If I can talk to her and get answers..." She choked up before she could finish.

"Rayla ... this must be eating you alive." He squeezed her a bit tighter. "I'm so sorry. Is there anything I can do?"

Rayla tipped her head upward from the crook of his neck and laid a kiss on his jaw. "Just your being here and knowing the whole story helps, Luke. But, now that I think about it, there is one more thing you can do."

"Name it."

"Help me get that moissanite gem out of the chandelier? Between my IPA and your FBI creds, we shouldn't have too much trouble getting the manager and security from the hotel to give us permission."

"Heck, they might even help if we ask," Luke replied.

"You're probably right. After that, I'd like to shelf everything that happened over this crazy weekend, at least for a while. If you're up for it, I'd love to show you the island."

"I'd like that a lot."

He wasn't wrong about obtaining the help. Security escorted them to the Cupola Bar, turned off the laser security system, and provided a stepladder for her to retrieve the moissanite stone.

Except, the moment Rayla had removed the egg-sized, multi-faceted gem from the chandelier, she was driven to examine it with her loupe. Something didn't seem right; it was too heavy. And sure enough, exactly as she suspected, the gem she held was not the moissanite fake.

It was the genuine Brilliant Oval, one-hundred-nineteen carat Maiden of St. Marys.

26

RAYLA STARED AT the diamond in her hand as her brain worked overtime, the electrical impulses skimming over synapses at lightning speed to help her understand what Gram had done.

The thief in her taking center stage, as usual, her first inclination was to figure out how her grandmother had perpetrated the reverse burglary, thus pushing the "why" and all ramifications that accompanied that question to the back of her mind.

Following those instincts, she first checked for the button cams she had planted the night before. Still in place, upon further examination, the two on the lower level—the ones that belonged to her had been fried with a laser. She imagined the two Luke and Dave had brought, which she had adhered upstairs, were likely in the same state. None would offer usable data on the perpetration.

Her eyes quickly flitted to each of the surveillance cams all around the lower floor. She knew from her own research and heist, the cams were wireless. She had bypassed them with still pictures rather than jamming them because she didn't want anyone aware there had been a burglary before the real thieves were able to perpetrate. Jamming the signals would replace the regular footage with static for the timeframe they had been blocked.

Gram, on the other hand, didn't have to worry about static on the footage or anyone becoming suspicious of a burglary. A signal jammer would have been a much faster way to disable the cams, and Rayla had little doubt that was what her grandmother had done.

Though sure she was right, to check her hypothesis, she queried the head of the security team. "Can you get one of your officers to take a look at the footage on these cameras from … um, say two to five this morning? Somewhere in there the stream should go to static for about ten to fifteen minutes."

"Yes, ma'am," the chief answered. "Perkins… Do as the lady requested," he said sweeping a hand from his officer to the door.

By the time the officer returned with her theory corroborated—twelve minutes of static on the surveillance cameras' feed from three-thirty-four to three-forty-six a.m.—Rayla had become marginally aware that Luke had summoned Grand's general manager to the Cupola Bar. After being informed of the latest events, the impeccably-dressed and poised lady phoned the island's chief of police and asked him to return. She also phoned Jaimeson Pinchot, the great, great, great grandson of Corporal John Pinchot and the current heir of the resplendent diamond.

Background goings-on filed in the recesses of her brain, Rayla's complete attention reverted to Gram's likely MO in replacing the diamond from where she, Rayla, had removed it.

After taking out the button cams with a high-powered laser, and incapacitating the surveillance cams with a signal jammer, Gram had to tackle the laser security within the display. Those were powered by electricity, and Rayla deduced Gram, though undoubtedly knowing where the nearest circuit breaker box was located for the Cupola Bar area, would not risk blacking out a significant region of the hotel to get to the diamond display. *She rerouted the lasers, same as I did.* In fact, the rest of Gram's reverse heist matched Rayla's step for step. Except, when the woman left, she had the moissanite rock in her pocket instead of The Maiden. Rayla flinched with that observation.

"Luke," she called out as she handed the diamond to Grand's general manager to be professionally authenticated. "There's GPS in the replica stone." With Luke on her heels, she converged on her room and whipped out her laptop. But, even as she ran with the hope of tracking her exceedingly thief-savvy grandmother, she knew the lady was too good not to have expected a tracker. The best thief Rayla knew, the thief who had trained her, would know her granddaughter had mandated the designer to include some type of GPS capability inside the moissanite stone. *Might as well find out where she ditched it.*

Pulling up the tracker's coordinates on her laptop, Rayla saw the fake diamond traveling at a pretty good clip, what her computer claimed to be around four-hundred-plus miles per hour and heading south out of Pellston. She couldn't help but laugh.

"She kept it with her, and she's headed for Detroit and then on to Paris?" Luke asked.

Rayla tamed her laugh to a smile. "I very much doubt the diamond's with her. If Gram had it, she'd have stored it in a lead-lined case so it couldn't be detected and she wouldn't be detained. More likely she planted it on Dave, and he *was* unknowingly transporting it." Her grin became a chuckle again. "Since he's on his way to Detroit from the Pellston airport, I'll bet he knows about it now."

27

Luke rose from the folding chair he'd been sitting in way too long, wanting nothing more than to massage his aching ass. Resisting the urge because of the females present, he walked around the general manager's office rubbing his face instead.

His eyelids hung like lead weights, barely open from lack of sleep and the boring rehashing of details that had taken up most of the day. Everyone involved—i.e., Mackinac Island's chief of police, the general manager and the executive vice president of Grand Hotel, and Jaimeson Pinchot, who resided on the island with his family during the summer season—pretty much demanded a minute by minute explanation regarding The Triple Crown challenge, the heisting of The Maiden, the return of The Maiden, and the FBI and IPA's take on all of it. The only bright spot was the humor that gurgled inside him every time one of them called Rayla "Detective Sergeant Rousseau." A laugh spurted out on one occasion, which awarded him a glare from his unamused girlfriend.

After the diamond had been satisfactorily authenticated, Pinchot, having heard all the details on Rayla's "IPA training," asked her to return the resplendent gem to its display. He was particularly grateful to have his diamond safe and sound and back in the Cupola Bar chandelier, but now that he knew it could be stolen with such ease, Rayla walked him through a series of added security measures that would help ensure its safety in the future.

Because of her extra time with Pinchot and the explanations and paperwork Grand's security and the island's chief of police required for their reports, it was dinnertime when Luke and Rayla finished with the group. The late hour denied them enough time to tour the island, and since Luke needed to get back to California for work on Monday, they'd have to fly out the next morning. Bummer, for sure.

Both famished because they'd missed lunch, he and Rayla converged on the Main Dining Room like a couple of half-starved alley cats the moment it opened for dinner at six-thirty p.m. After finding a relatively secluded corner where they could talk freely, albeit discreetly, their behinds had barely connected with the chair cushions when an unexpected yet very familiar face appeared, asking if she could join them.

Evie.

At that precise moment, Luke was unsure what he was going to do about the superlative thief, Evangeline Rousseau. He couldn't arrest her or allow her to be outed for any of the thefts ... not if he wanted to remain an FBI agent, not to mention a free man. If Evie was caught, his house of cards would tumble right along with hers.

As well as his own dilemma with the Robin(s) matriarch, he also had no idea how Rayla would react to her grandmother's presence here, but *he* certainly wouldn't deny Evie the right to dine with them. He rose, circled the table, and held out a chair for Rayla's criminally precocious grandmother.

A glance at Rayla revealed his girlfriend appeared to be in a state of shock. *This could get awkward. Very, very awkward.*

Luke returned to his seat and began the difficult conversation they all knew they must have with a wisp of humor.

"So ... Evie ... What's new with you?"

The woman snickered, but Rayla dove past the pleasantries, her facial features gargoyle-like and her tone caustic—a side of her Luke had rarely seen.

"You sent me here knowing I'd steal The Maiden to better protect her, while all along intending to steal her from me? I can't begin to wrap my head around those reprehensible actions. How many rules of theft did you break to arrive at this disgraceful low in your thieving career?"

"Quite a few, dear, I'm sure," Evie answered.

"Just to get us all on the same page," Luke interrupted, "you are the burglar of all three diamonds in the Triple Crown of Jewel Theft, correct? Oh, wait. Would you like me to read you your rights, first?"

"Not necessary, Special Agent Keltry. You won't be arresting me; we all know that. To answer your question, yes. I am the thief of The Lynx, The Contessa, and the second thief of The Maiden of St. Mary's, having removed it from Special Agent Knapp's room earlier this morning after Rayla stole it from its display. However, at this time, The Lynx and The Contessa are on their way back to their countries where they will arrive safe and sound to be restored to their specific exhibitory displays tomorrow morning. And, of course, you know all about The Maiden's status."

Luke's chin jutted upward. "How are The Lynx and Contessa being returned? You're here."

Evie grinned. She wouldn't be offering an explanation, at least not yet.

Luke plunged forward with the rest of the suppositions and questions that had been bubbling up in his federally-focused brain since he'd discovered Evie had been the thief. "You weren't in Paris when I called you that Tuesday morning before I flew back to LA from Michigan. You were already in Cape Town." Not a question, but Evie's whereabouts at that time required affirmation before he could move on.

"That's correct," Evie answered, "nor when Rayla called while I was talking to you,"

Rayla lobbed her attention between the two of them, finally landing on Luke. "You called her after I dropped you at the airport? Why?"

Luke stared back, waffling with what he should say.

Evie answered for him. "Luke had some questions and observations about your father, Rayla. Fed-savvy observations he wasn't sure he should share with you."

Rayla's unholy glare took a momentary respite, her lips splitting in a knowing smile which she pitched toward him. "You picked up on my dad's thieving inclinations and probably the fact he knows about mine, as well?"

"Uh—"

"You didn't think I knew about Gram and Gramp training him or the fact he knows I'm a member of the Robin(s) or *Thief à la Femme*? You were wrong, Luke. I've known since shortly after I began training with *her*." She flipped her once again disapproving gaze on Evie. "All these years you and dad have been trying to protect me, or maybe it would be more accurate to say you were trying to protect Mom. But she knows, too; she always has. She and I made a pact, right here on Mackinac Island as it turns out, when we came here after I spent my seventh summer with you in Paris—the same year you invited me to join the Robin(s). Mom knew all about my dad, you, and Gramp and your careers as thieves before she and dad married. When she saw the diamond I earned from opening the jewelry box that summer with you in Paris, she knew you'd asked me to train and join the sisterhood. Camille Johnson-Rousseau is so much more intelligent than you and my dad have ever given her credit."

Evie's mouth was slightly ajar, something Luke had never before witnessed. *I didn't think anyone could get the upper hand on this lady.* For sure, if anyone could, it would be Rayla. And his gorgeous, sexy, thief of a girlfriend just did.

"I'm sure we're going to have quite the eye-opening family reunion when Mom and Dad return from Bangladesh, but I'm more interested in your explanation for going over to the dark side—if, in fact, there is one."

"There is, Rayla. That's why I'm here. I wanted the opportunity to explain all of this to you, and to, hopefully, attain your understanding."

Luke looked over to see Rayla's fiery gaze, fixed unswervingly on her grandmother, blaze ever hotter.

"Not my forgiveness?" Rayla asked, her anger burning so hot it reddened her cheeks. Luke swore the temperature in the room rose several degrees, as well.

"No, Rayla. I *do not* want forgiveness, wouldn't take it if you offered it. I had to do what I did. If I had it all to do over, I wouldn't change a thing."

The rigidity of Rayla's features and the fire in her eyes increased, white hot and hardening and blazing more with each passing second. *Is it possible Evie is purposely stoking Rayla's rage?*

"Letting me steal The Maiden and then stealing it from me included?" Rayla queried through clenched teeth.

"Especially that. Once I knew I couldn't keep you from coming up here on your 'save The Maiden' crusade, there was no way for me to steal that diamond. If I was going to get it, it had to be from you."

Luke certainly understood that logic, and he was sure Rayla had, too, but the unacceptability of Evie's actions in perpetrating these thefts remained the still unanswered point of contention.

"If you'd like to hear my side of this disagreeable matter, I'm ready to tell you. If not, I'll be on my way home to Paris." She fixed her eyes on Luke. "You have no evidence to support arresting me for these thefts, other than the confession I just made which, unless you recorded it, something I strongly doubt, is not enough to take to the DOJ. All the diamonds will be returned, and you can't place me at any of the crime scenes—not even Agent Knapp's room. Besides that, your attempt to pin these crimes on me will end your career and dissolve the Robin(s) of the Hood. I have always believed you to be an intelligent man and an FBI agent of highest integrity, Luke. I can't imagine you would change your opinion of the Robin(s) or sacrifice your career, not to mention your own freedom, because of these actions—which no longer bear any consequence."

Luke again stole a glance at Rayla. If he knew her the way he thought he did, she wanted to hear Evie's explanation, but she was too proud to admit it. Not a problem. He was more than willing to be the one to ask.

"I'd like to hear your explanation, Evie," he said. "But, I'd like to do so as your granddaughter's boyfriend ... and your friend ... not as an FBI agent." He unrolled his silverware from its napkin, furtively removed his creds and gun from his belt—wrapping them quickly in the napkin out of sight on his lap—and handed the heavy-laden napkin to Evie under the table.

The lady graciously accepted the smartly concealed implements, keeping them out of sight, but she didn't start talking. First, she locked eyes with Rayla. Only when her granddaughter proffered a slight nod, did Evie begin.

"For your sake, Luke, I'm going back a lot farther than Rayla likely needs. Back to a past that haunts me to this day."

28

GRAM'S REVELATION ABOUT the history lesson for Luke's sake seized her attention like a sparkling diamond in a jewelry store window ... *or, perhaps a brand-new Corvette?* Rayla thought she knew immediately where her grandmother would begin this tale, but she was wrong. Gram went back much farther, at long last bestowing information Rayla had never completely known. She eagerly lapped up every drop of the intel her grandmother bestowed like an animal who'd been given water for the first time in days.

"The Triple Crown of Jewel Theft thieving challenge was penned fifty years ago on July 5th ... by my husband on his twenty-second birthday, along with his older brother, Adrien, four years before I met and ran away with Étienne."

Rayla's eyes bugged out of their sockets and she coughed, practically choking on her own saliva. "Gramp?" she uttered in disbelief. "Gramp instigated that horrible challenge? Why?"

"Your grandfather was a thief in every sense of the word, Rayla," Gram answered. "Not stealing from the poor was the only high-end moral to which he'd ever adhered. Everyone and everything else were fair game to him and his family. When I came along, and he'd taught me the art of theft, I attempted to instill more honor in him, but I never totally got through.

"Étienne lusted after diamonds in particular, although anything that could be stolen put a glimmer in his eye. Thankfully, he had no problem with my desire to turn the training he'd lavished upon me into a worthwhile cause, something that could be used for the good of humanity. He admired that venerable quality in me, though try as he might, he couldn't share my enthusiasm for it. Nevertheless, he was extremely helpful in setting up the Robin(s) of the Hood and even did a few jobs with us to further assist Patti and me in getting the sisterhood up and running." She stopped and looked off somewhat wistfully.

"Eliot was twelve when he found out his father and uncle had created the challenge, and that was the point when he decided not to follow in our thieving footsteps. He confided to me he wanted nothing to do with his father's illicit lifestyle. He accepted, even condoned, my *Robin Hood* approach, but didn't agree with Étienne's purely thief persona.

"Your father had excellent grades in school and made maintaining those grades his priority from that point on. His educational diligence during his *lycée*, or high school years, allowed him to qualify for scholarships to several American universities. He chose the University of Michigan and the pre-med major and left the day after his high school graduation. Though he remained in touch with me, he was hardly civil toward his father. As I said, Eliot was okay with what I was doing, but he hadn't had a meaningful relationship with his father since he had discovered Étienne and Adrien had penned that dreadful challenge."

"I never knew any of this," Rayla said.

"That's the way your father wanted it, Rayla. He didn't want there to be any friction between you and your grandfather because Camille had been so grateful for our help with you. She desperately wanted to continue her pre-med education. She leapt at my offer to come to Michigan and help out. Eliot went along, but Étienne wasn't part of the deal. Eliot refused to welcome his father into your Stateside home."

Rayla suddenly realized the truth of that statement. Gramp had never visited them in Michigan while she was growing up. She only ever saw him summers in Paris and Nice, and never had she seen her father and grandfather together. She'd always thought Gramp simply hadn't wanted to leave Europe, and her dad hadn't wanted to return there.

"Getting back to The Triple Crown challenge," Gram continued, "it wasn't the big deal my husband and his brother had hoped. There were only a few attempts in the first few years to cash in on the reward—a sizable amount which the two of them had arranged to be paid out by a local fence in Paris with them getting a percentage of the profit. None completed the challenge. A few had been able to steal The Lynx, and fewer still The Lynx and The Contessa, but no one had been successful in nabbing The Maiden."

The gleam in her grandmother's eye was undeniable, and Rayla caught on quickly. "You? You foiled all heist attempts on The Maiden?" Her mouth remained open as she expelled a breath of incredulity and awe. It was true the magnificent gem had never been stolen. Endeavors were made over the years, but all were thwarted, always with the thieves getting caught red-handed. "But, how was that possible? You didn't even know Gramp then. You would have only been twelve."

"By God's grace, I suppose, The Maiden remained untouched for the first five years of the challenge. A year after Étienne and I were married, when I had mastered the fine art of theft over and above what my husband had hoped, an almost successful heist stirred me to become involved in protecting The Maiden of St. Marys."

"Of course. You knew when a thief or thieves were going after The Maiden because the other two diamonds had already been stolen."

"True, but there were also attempts made on The Maiden alone. I've always loved that diamond as much as you, Rayla. I grew up in Michigan, too, and my family also vacationed on this island regularly. So, I put my own alarm system in place on that gem a year after Étienne and I were married."

A stunned expression still on her face, Rayla glanced at Luke who was equally enthralled. "So there's another alarm system on that diamond which I didn't see when I lifted it?" Rayla asked. "But how..."

"Yes, dear, there is. You couldn't possibly have spotted it, so please don't be too hard on yourself." She raised both hands to stop Rayla from finishing her question. "I disconnected the silent alarm before you stole the diamond, honey. Obviously, I didn't want you caught.

"I began my crusade to keep The Maiden safe by perpetrating a heist on the gem in the area in which it was displayed at that time. There, I placed a state-of-the-art, advanced technology motion alarm woven into the navy velvet pedestal on which the diamond rested. I patched the sensor's silent alarm into the wiring of the other alarms within the display. Any theft attempt activated an audio alarm which sounded in the security guards' monitoring room, but one that was silent at the display. The thieves were unaware they had been outed until security was upon them. That's why they all were caught.

"When the Pinchots had the diamond moved into the chandelier they had designed in the Cupola Bar at the time that area was completed in 1987, I instigated another perpetration there and upgraded with an updated motion detection sensor. That one was crystal clear, and it blended invisibly into the clear glass pedestal of the new display. Before your theft, the first little number and its updated cousin have been alerting security at this hotel of thefts in progress on The Maiden of St. Marys for the last forty-five years without fail. That's why those damn thugs were caught every time."

"And Gramp never knew?" Rayla asked.

"If he did, he didn't let on, but I honestly don't believe he was aware. He attempted to steal The Maiden a couple years later, you know, to determine why those thieves, some of the best in the business, couldn't do it. Knowing he was going after it, I followed him and set off another audio alarm with enough time for him to get away. After that, I thought he'd given up on anyone completing the challenge."

"But he decided to take it on himself," Rayla said in barely a whisper.

Gram nodded. "I thought you might have put that together. On the thirty-fourth anniversary of the challenge, he and his brother Adrien decided to prove to the world they were the best by successfully perpetrating the three thefts, their goal to complete the challenge before its thirty-fifth anniversary. At that point, nobody had so much as tried in fifteen years."

"But——" Rayla started.

"I tried to talk him out of it, even attempted to reason with Adrien, to no avail," Gram cut in. "They were both hellbent on the glory of completing the very challenge they had created— even though the fence with whom they had the agreement refused to pay out to them as the thieves. Without their personal mover, they couldn't hope to get even a third of what the diamonds were worth, but they didn't care. All that mattered anymore was that they would be heralded as the only thieves who could do it."

"But Gramp had already determined The Maiden couldn't be stolen. Why would he believe anything had changed?"

"He said having Adrien along would make all the difference. He even asked me to help, though he knew how reprehensible I found the whole business. Of course I refused."

"What would you have done if he'd managed to make it to The Maiden that time, Gram?"

"Certainly what I'd done before, but I didn't have to face the problem. As you already guessed, Rayla, Étienne died from internal injuries he accrued when he fell from the fourth story of the Cape Town Museum before he and Adrien were able to breach the building. Adrien got them out of Cape Town, flying them home to Paris by way of a privately chartered jet.

"I pleaded with Adrien to take him to the hospital there in Cape Town, but your stubborn grandfather wouldn't permit it. He said the police were already onto the heist when Adrien got them to the safety of the jet, that Interpol was on top of the attempt to complete The Triple Crown challenge. He claimed their appearance at the Cape Town museum was the reason he'd lost his footing and fell, though I knew better. He said they'd know for sure how he'd sustained his injuries if he were hospitalized.

"Once they were back in Paris, I called in a doctor friend, but Étienne needed surgery for any hope to survive. The doctor could do nothing. Your grandfather was under surveillance throughout Europe for various high-end burglaries, and a warrant had gone out for his arrest in connection with the theft of The Lynx and attempted theft of The Contessa. So even in Paris, he wouldn't allow me to take him to the hospital. I nursed him as best I could, but he died two days after the fall."

She laid her face in her hands for a silent moment. When she lifted her head, she turned away from them. "Such a fool. Although he was only fifty-six, he had been diagnosed with Parkinson's Disease two years earlier. He hadn't perpetrated a heist since his diagnosis … well, none that I know of, anyway. He must have felt compelled to take on that one last challenge, needing to believe he still had what it took to pull off those last flawless heists." She faced Rayla and Luke. "The evening after he died, I boxed up and mailed The Lynx back to the museum in Trondheim."

When Gram appeared to be finished explaining, Luke breathed out an audible sigh. "That doesn't explain your actions in stealing them now, Evie," he said.

"Before he died, Étienne asked Adrien to promise he'd complete the challenge. Adrien laughed at him, saying he had never been the thief Étienne had been, and he certainly wasn't capable of completing the challenge without his brother's help. But my headstrong husband made him promise he'd find someone to help him do it. Then he turned to me and made me vow I would see it done if no one had taken up the gauntlet by the time the challenge turned fifty."

"And you agreed?" Rayla said, her disbelief framed in a penetrating gawk.

"He was dying in my arms, honey. I couldn't refuse him his final wish. I honestly didn't intend to keep the promise. And, all these years later, I'd forgotten about it. But Adrien hadn't. He turned seventy-six this year, and that old fart contacted me, said he was bound by his oath as 'a thief and a gentleman' to see to his brother's final wish. When I *wished him* luck, he said he'd get his son to help him if I wouldn't. Adrien's son is fifty-five, and he couldn't steal a wallet if it fell out of a mark's pocket. I knew Adrien would get involved, and I didn't want to bear any responsibility for his death or imprisonment, so ... here we are."

"With all three diamonds back in their displays, there won't be a collection on the reward," Luke said.

"That was my deal with Adrien. He and I never promised Étienne we would collect the reward, only that we'd complete the challenge. So, I told my brother-in-law I'd steal all three stones, let him hold them, get some memorable pictures of all three together, and have the thefts verified by the press. I also told him he'd get the credit for The Triple Crown thefts in the thieving community, thus ending the challenge. I'd make sure of it. But then all the gems were going back where they belonged. As I said, The Lynx and The Contessa should arrive at their respective museums tomorrow morning, and you know the situation with The Maiden."

Luke whipped out his phone. Checking Evie's claim via news sites, he showed Rayla the confirmation that all three diamonds had been stolen. "Adrien was or still is here? That's the only way he'd have been able to hold all three."

"He was here ... briefly. He flew onto the island yesterday and spent the night in my room. After I snatched The Maiden

175

from Agent Knapp's room, we took the pictures and uploaded them to a popular news site via an untraceable IP address. Then I accompanied him, The Lynx, and The Contessa on a chartered flight to Pellston. I put Adrien on a plane to Detroit with a connection to Paris and dropped the well-packaged diamonds off at FedEx. I made special provisions for them to be delivered to their prospective museums tomorrow, Sunday, by paying a criminally exorbitant fee for Extra-Priority Overnight Air and the Sunday delivery. Then, I came back here to talk with you.

"Didn't trust him to return the two diamonds?" Luke asked.

Evie grinned. "Let's just say I thought it best not to tempt him."

"Why'd you go through all the trouble of putting The Maiden back in its display? Why not leave it on the general manager's desk, since you were right here?"

"I can answer that," Rayla said. "She still wants to keep dirty, grubby, thieving paws off The Maiden, so she updated the motion detector to the latest model and made sure it was in place when she reinstated the diamond in its display." Another moment's thought and she added, "But you had to know I'd remove it when I went back for the moissanite stone and discovered The Maiden there instead, and the owner would want the diamond reauthenticated."

"I did. As you said, my primary reason for returning the diamond to the chandelier was to update the detection system I had on the pedestal." She grinned mischievously. "Although, I have to admit, imagining your reaction when you discovered the real Maiden instead of your fake was a delightful concept."

With their reciprocating smiles, she continued, "I didn't connect the silent alarm to the security system until after the diamond had been authenticated and I was sure it was back in its display. Your telling Pinchot to add a silent alarm similar to mine for extra security on the diamond will double the diamond's protection now."

176

"How'd you get into the security monitoring room to reconnect the silent alarm in broad daylight with officers everywhere?" Luke asked.

Rayla tossed him a disbelieving gape. "Really, Luke?"

Gram laughed, but went ahead and explained it for Luke's less-than-thief-savvy brain. "Security was all over the Cupola Bar area, but no one was in the monitoring room. I slipped in and connected my device into their wireless system while the officers were otherwise occupied." She eyed Rayla with a smile. "By the way, dear, your theft of The Maiden was exquisite—every bit the consummate burglary I expect from the world's foremost female thief."

"I learned from the best," Rayla responded with a grin. "But, how did you watch my theft?"

"Same as Agent Knapp. I piggybacked off the FBI button cam Luke planted."

29

"You'll never guess what security found when they X-rayed my carryon bag at the Pellston Regional Airport," Dave said in lieu of a greeting for his early Sunday morning call.

Luke knew the answer, but he played dumb. "Uh, spare magazine for your weapon? You really should have declared it, or better yet, kept it with you and your creds."

"It wasn't a magazine. What they found looked like The Maiden of St. Marys diamond. They detained me until I proved I was FBI and some gem authenticator they called determined the rock was fake. Even then, they had a ton of questions. I convinced them to call Lt. Saber to back me. Embarrassing, especially after the way I treated her. I was glad her cellphone was included on the card she gave me."

"Let this be a lesson to you. Always the nice guy, no matter what." He held the phone away from his mouth so Dave wouldn't hear him laugh, but it didn't matter. His boss had him pegged.

"I know you're laughing, Luke. Don't try to fight it. It's damn funny, even to me."

Luke put the phone back to his mouth and gurgled out the last of his humor.

"I would like to be filled in, though. I was informed when I arrived in Detroit that the real diamond reappeared in its display. Do you, your girlfriend, and/or her boss have any idea what happened, why the diamond was returned or how the fake got into my bag?"

"Not a clue, but thanks for letting us know what happened to the fake. We thought the thief took it as a consolation prize." He'd definitely improved in the fine art of lying, especially to his superior, over the last couple of days. "We spent all day yesterday walking through everything with Grand Hotel's chief of security, general manager, executive vice president, the owner of the diamond, and Mackinac Island's chief of police—all the powers that be. Nobody can so much as guess why the diamond was returned. And here's another nugget for you. The other two diamonds from the heist challenge, The Levanger Lynx and The Contessa of Kimberley, showed up via special FedEx deliveries at their museums this morning, so we figure that plays in somehow."

"Really?" Dave asked. "So, somebody just stole them to say they had?"

"That's what it looks like," Luke answered.

"That's incredible. One of those mysteries we'll probably never figure out. I suspect that drives IPA as crazy as it does us." He sighed. "Anyway, I wanted to let you know you can stay an extra couple of days up there if you'd like. There was apparently a snafu when they put the roof on our newly renovated Ventura office and some gusty winds caught the tiles just right and blew them and half the roof off the building. The roofers need everybody out at least through Tuesday to conduct the repairs."

"Anything inside damaged?"

"Thankfully, no. Only most of the roof is gone."

"That is fabulous news," Luke blurted. "I mean about the extended vacation, not the roof. I'm glad you called. Rayla and I were packing up to hop a flight off the island. Hopefully, we'll be able to extend our stay here at Grand, which means I'll get the scenic tour of Mackinac Island she promised me."

"I take it you were able to talk things through and all is well between the two of you, then?"

"We stayed up most of last night talking about how our particular careers sometimes require calculated dishonesty. We decided what we have is worth it, and we're going forward. Sometimes one or the other of us won't be able to fill the other in, but at least now we know why, and that makes it acceptable."

"Glad to hear it, Luke. I know it didn't start out this way, but once I found out she was law enforcement, I was pulling for you."

"I appreciate that," Luke responded, but deep inside, the double standard was taking its toll. *If it stops here, if I don't have to lie to Dave or anyone anymore. I can live with it.* But who was he kidding? The chances of that were pretty slim.

While Luke was on the phone with Dave, Rayla took the opportunity to call Devon. She'd promised her bestie an update as soon as she had one, but after everything that transpired yesterday, and with the knowledge of Gram's involvement, she didn't feel much like running through it again. Good thing, too, because sometime during the remainder of Saturday night—after she left the island bound for Amy's in Santa Monica to conduct an update meeting with the rest of the Robin(s)—Rayla and Luke decided nobody else needed to know the specifics about The Triple Crown thefts, especially the part about Gram being the thief. If her grandmother wanted to tell the others, that was her business. The sisterhood wouldn't be made privy by either her or Luke.

With that decision uppermost in her mind, and upon overhearing she and Luke were going to have another couple of days on the island, she tapped out Devon's number in the burner phone she was using. She greeted her groggy-sounding friend as she realized the time difference made it a bit early for Devon.

"Hey…" she said, her tone apologetic. "I'm sorry I'm calling so early. I forgot you're three-hours behind me."

"It's okay," Devon answered. "I'm glad to hear from you. You're okay, right?"

"A little tired, but other than that I'm fine."

"I expected a call yesterday, and when I didn't get one, I was a little concerned. I tried to call you several times. When you didn't pick up and the phone went straight to voicemail, I hoped you'd accidently let the battery die. Was that what happened?"

"Yeah, sorry. I found it dead this morning and charged it. I was afraid you might be worried, but yesterday was crazy. By the time we'd finished with all the local authorities, I couldn't face going through it again. I figure I owe you an explanation now."

"For sure you do! What happened? Was Deidre helpful?"

"That's the understatement of the year. If she hadn't shown up when she did, I'd be on my way to a federal lockup, probably in DC. As things stand, Special Agent Dave Knapp believes I'm Detective Sergeant Rayla Rousseau, an undercover detective for the International Police Alliance operating out of Santa Barbara. That's what he'll always need to believe from this point on. Oh, by the way. My job as COO at ARI is my cover job for the IPA position now—at least with Dave and the FBI." She pitched her eyes upward. "Bet you never thought that job would end up covering for two careers. I know I didn't."

Devon chuckled. "Never really thought about it, but it doesn't surprise me. Your life is beyond complicated, Ray."

"Boy, you can say that again. If I overheard correctly while Luke was talking to his boss just now, Dave is so relieved I turned out to be a LEO, he's given Luke his blessing to pursue a relationship with me. Talk about ironic."

Devon shared a laugh with her. "So, what exactly happened up there yesterday? Last I knew from you, you were waiting for the real burglar to snatch your fake gem and called me to send Deidre just in case things didn't go right. Then we saw a news clip yesterday that claimed all three gems had been successfully stolen. We assumed the burglar had your moissanite fake, not the real diamond. Then another news report stated the real Maiden of St. Marys was back in its display."

After explaining the series of events leading up to her arrest by Luke's boss, except leaving out the identity of the thief, Rayla informed Devon about the other news reports which aired that morning—ones none of the sisterhood would have seen yet—asserting The Levanger Lynx and The Contessa of Kimberley had also been returned to their rightful homes. Rayla confirmed the accuracy of those reports.

"But you never caught or even saw the thief?" Devon asked.

"Seriously bad-ass criminal or, more likely, criminals," Rayla responded. "The heists were way too smooth to have been perpetrated by a single thief. We never saw a trace of them. We finally concluded, whoever they were, all they wanted was the glory of the successful burglaries on the fiftieth anniversary of the challenge. Having proven they had done it, the diamonds were returned." She held her breath and hoped like hell that would appease her friend. Thankfully, it did.

Lying to Devon was up there on the "list of her most hated things," but as she had determined with Luke's friends and family, when you're a thief, lies are a given—even with your own friends and family.

"Are you on your way back?" Devon asked.

"Actually, no. Luke just talked to Dave and he's got another two-day reprieve because of wind damage to the FBI office in Ventura. We're staying, and I'm going to give him the 'Rayla Rousseau' grand tour of the island."

"Sounds fun and romantic, but before you lose yourselves on Mackinac Island, can the Robin(s) borrow the both of you on a video hangout?"

"Sure. What's up?"

"Except for you, we're all here at my mom's for the debrief meeting from our last two jobs, and we've run into a little ... *situation* ... concerning Special Agents Barb Sutherlin and Deb Sines."

30

"EVERYBODY STOP TALKING!" Luke yelled. He skimmed the faces of each of the Robin(s) gathered at Amy's ocean-beach home in Santa Monica, visible through Rayla's laptop by way of an encrypted video hangout the ladies had developed. Rayla sat next to him in the Cupola suite at Grand Hotel, which they'd managed to keep for their extended stay. Try though he did, however, he couldn't stop himself from holding Evie's gaze for several seconds. With a reassuring smile for her and a little effort, he cleared his head of the weekend's events and eyed the remainder of the group clustered on or around a leather sofa. "One of you start from the beginning and tell me what's going on."

All the women swung their heads toward Tarry. She swallowed hard, as if a little fearful about what she was about to impart to him.

Since Devon had told Rayla it was him they needed to talk to, Luke hoped they again needed Bureau help with a Robin(s)' mission. Unfortunately, since Devon had said there was some kind of situation going on with Barb and Deb, that pointed to something else entirely. As he regarded the group of somber-faced women on the screen before him, his head spun with an unhealthy helping of dread. This didn't bode well.

Momentarily, Patti, sitting next to Tarry on the sofa, took the second-generation Robin(s)' hand in hers. "We've landed ourselves in this dilemma because Tarry and I bumped into Barb last week at your office, Luke. In retrospect, we all agree,

185

none of us should have gone there in the first place. But I think I can speak for Tarry, as well, when I say I don't feel we should bear the burden alone." She scanned the others. "We're all in this together, ladies, like it or not. The least you can do is back us up." She glanced around at the others, and one by one, they nodded.

What the hell happened over there? They were all behaving as if they'd prefer facing a judge for their crimes rather than him. "Fine," Luke responded. "Just speak one at a time, okay?"

The roomful of Robin(s) exchanged enigmatic glances while Tarry cleared her throat.

"Barb and those of us she knows sort of got together again, you know, to catch up ... like old friends do."

"Sort of?" he questioned.

"Okay, we did. Barb contacted me right after we saw her on Monday and the first two generations of Robin(s)—those of us who knew her minus Evie, who was doing a job in Europe—met her for lunch on Tuesday. We had a great time. It was fun catching up with her."

She looked around the room for confirmation and waited for her comrades to acknowledge before continuing. "We had four missions on the docket for the weekend which split our group. Patti, Devon, Tami, Wendy, and I took down a crooked insurance agency in Atlanta, while Amy, Jodi, Krista, Laura, and Katherine dealt with a Ponzi scheme in Houston. As I said, Evie was doing a solo job in Europe, and Rayla went to Mackinac Island on a personal mission as *Thief à la Femme*. Except for Evie and Rayla, we were all back by Friday night, and we met for drinks in Santa Barbara."

"Because you all flew into Santa Barbara?" Luke questioned.

"That's right. We prearranged the get-together and then set up our flight schedules to bring both our crews back to California via SBA."

"I'm with you so far," Luke said. "Go on."

Tarry exhaled a heavy, trepidation-fraught sigh, and hesitated.

Devon came to her rescue. "I told Rayla we saw Special Agent Sines committing a B&E on our way to the bar. Did she tell you, Luke?"

"Rayla said you told her Sines was a damn good burglar who'd done the community a service by robbing a filthy-rich congressman who also happens to be a miserable reprobate."

Devon's smile lit up the computer screen. "One or the other of you added a little more to my intel, but that's pretty accurate." She chuckled. "I didn't talk to Rayla again after that conversation until she called me a while ago this morning, so we didn't know whether she'd told you, or if she had, how you'd responded. As thieves ourselves, we never intended to out her. We consider her a high-end thief in good standing. But since Rayla told you, we need to know if you told Special Agent Sutherlin, and if so, how she reacted, and what you intend to do, if anything."

"I didn't tell Sutherlin, or anyone," he said. "To be honest, I hadn't really given it a lot of thought one way or the other. We were in the middle of our own boatload of crap over here when Rayla told me. Anyway, I didn't see Deb commit the B&E, so I have no firsthand intel. Considering she's FBI, and occupying the office space next to mine, I have an interest but certainly no intention of ratting her out. I suspect the local police are handling it if the congressman reported the burglary. What's your concern with this?"

Tarry inhaled a cavernous breath. "The situation has become more complicated because it turns out everything Barb told us at the park when you were with us was a lie, Luke, or half-truths at best. Laura picked up some chatter through one of our dark web sites. There was another burglary later Friday night, committed by two female thieves. Laura got us into the conversation, and the chat room groupies said the congressman's burglary and the one perpetrated later that night on a Santa Barbara judge were both accomplished by a female duo that's been around for several years, only they had always worked the LA area."

"Okay. But I don't see how that's pertinent to me," Luke said.

"There's more," Laura picked up. "We were able to attain additional information on this duo from our dark web chatterers. We're well covered on the various sites we troll, so we were able to converse with them without concern, and we continued our fact-finding mission on the two lady thieves."

Luke's head wagged with his inability to comprehend. "Why would you do that? What's your interest in them? Even if one is Deb Sines, I don't understand why you'd care."

"Getting to that," Laura replied. "While we were chatting, intel came in about a burglary going down at that very minute on a snooty old couple up the beach a ways from Amy's here in Santa Monica."

"Luke, long story short, we lit out of here and watched the theft," Tarry said. "There's no doubt in our minds it was the blond we saw Friday, and this time she was with her partner ... Barb Sutherlin."

"What? Are you absolutely sure it was Sutherlin?" Luke asked, disbelief coursing within him.

"We're sure. Sorry, Luke," Devon said. "We have them on close-range video. It's Barb Sutherlin for sure with Deb Sines. And get this. According to the chat site, they're calling themselves Female Burglars, Inc."

His head sailed backward. "FBI..." he whispered.

31

"WHAT ARE YOU going to do about Barb and Deb?" Rayla asked as she and Luke exited their room, setting out for their tour of the island.

She almost hated to ask. Luke's original concept for dealing with her and the Robin(s) was spinning out of control, likely into areas he'd never intended to trod. He'd been notably quiet since their video chat with the rest of the Robin(s). *Maybe telling me how he's feeling will help him come to terms with it all.*

"I'm not sure," Luke answered. "I'd like to talk it out with them, but honestly, Rayla, what can I do? They've got just as much dirt on me as I have on them, at least according to Bureau standards. I can't out them— not that I would, anyway. In truth, the three of us are on the same page as far as I'm concerned. After all, I took the extra step, not a whole lot different than what they're doing. At first I planned to turn a blind eye to your activities, but then we agreed to help each other when a case called for it. The *FBI thieves* and I aren't different at all. I am sorry Sutherlin apparently didn't feel she could tell me the whole story when we talked at lunch that day, though."

"She still hid her full agenda. Why do you suppose she felt she needed to do that?"

Luke took her hand as they skimmed down the stairs to the Parlor. "No idea. I thought it was 'all cards on the table' that day. I have to believe she doesn't trust me." He opened the outside door, and they traversed the red-carpeted stairs to the sidewalk. Once there, he said, "I'll deal with it when we get home, hon. For now, I just want to enjoy paradise with you."

Paradise. For sure that should have been the name of this island. Luke couldn't remember when he had enjoyed himself half as much as he had today, riding horseback, biking, and walking around this eight-mile-circumference chunk of land in the middle of the Straits of Mackinac with his beautiful girlfriend.

Although they didn't get out the door until noon because of the need to work through registration to extend their stay, move him into Rayla's Cupola suite, and take care of the video chat with the Robin(s), Rayla still managed to show him everything that was important to her.

First, they rode rented bikes around an honest-to-goodness numbered Michigan highway that circled the island with a beautiful view of two of the Great Lakes all around—Lake Michigan beyond the bridge, and Lake Huron next to them on the island. During the ride, they stopped several times: once to climb up a humungous hill which provided a view from a rock ledge that was beyond phenomenal; once to build a stone tower to add to the gazillion already constructed by the lake; twice to wade into the lake and splash each other until they were drenched; and once at the halfway point to use the facilities and buy some ice cream.

After returning the bikes, they toured a butterfly sanctuary, various churches and museums, took a two-hour carriage ride throughout the interior of the island, and saw a real fort preserved from the 18th century. A significant climb up what felt more like a mountain than a hill, the fort featured actors dressed in military and time-period attire, and he and Rayla arrived in time to witness the booming of the canon. They also saw the Governor's Mansion—a summer place of respite for the residing governor of Michigan—and many other stately mansions and cottages in the upper hills of the island. He couldn't remember the names of most of the places Rayla had taken him, but she'd spared no expense. Six hours later, he was sure he'd seen the entire island.

For dinner, they ate at one of the more upper-class bistros on Main Street, then bought some famous Mackinac Island fudge. They sat by the lapping water of Lake Huron, indulging in the chocolate treat while watching the sun set beyond the Mackinac Bridge. The perfect end to a perfect day.

Throughout the day, they had talked and laughed a lot. But it wasn't until the sun had disappeared beyond the western horizon and they were walking back to the hotel that the conversation took a serious turn. Call it divine intervention, fate, or whatever, it seemed like too much of a coincidence that the pastor from the little stone church located just down the hill from Grand Hotel was out greeting Sunday evening attendees as they departed, and Rayla made an "off-hand comment" about that being the church she'd always imagined for her wedding.

Without a second thought, Luke guided them across the street and approached the clergyman. When the last couple had departed, the man turned a grinning face on them.

"I have a feeling I know why you've come over," he said, his smile widening. "It's generally quite a lengthy process to reserve this church for nuptials, and I'm afraid we are all booked through the remainder of the season."

"Even a spur of the moment elopement right now?" Luke asked. His grin became outright laughter at Rayla's disbelieving gawk.

"Right now?" the minister asked. "Do you have a marriage license from Mackinac County?" His lips split again with his endearing smile. "If you can provide that, I would be very happy to marry you tonight."

"We don't have the marriage license, pastor, but I believe I can remedy that situation, if you're willing to do the honors of performing the ceremony on such short notice."

"Perhaps you don't know the process, young man. It takes approximately seventy-two hours to have your marriage application approved and a license granted on this island; in fact, anywhere in Michigan."

"I think I know a way to expedite the process, sir. If I can manage it, are you willing to do an evening elopement ceremony tonight?"

The minister appeared perplexed, but eagerly nodded. "I am willing, indeed, and more than a little curious as to how you would accomplish this feat."

Luke returned a smile. "One minute, if you please."

With a grin stretching from ear to ear, he held both of Rayla's hands and turned her to face him. Dropping to one knee, he managed to get through his unrehearsed spiel without faltering or laughing at the absurdity of proposing to his untraditional girlfriend in such a traditional way.

"Rayla Lynn Rousseau, will you marry me ... here, now ... in the church you have always dreamed you'd be married in?"

To say her head spun would have been accurate but significantly more toned down than she felt.

Is he really doing this? Is Luke not only asking me to marry him, but expecting me to elope with him on the spot? She glanced downward at her attire ... *in jeans and a sweatshirt? And how's he planning to get this marriage license?* Her head toggled ever so slightly.

There wasn't a doubt in her mind about accepting his proposal, but the elopement ... here and now ... *That*, she wasn't sure about at all.

When a little too much time elapsed after his question, he squeezed her hands and repeated her name. "Rayla? A little too spur of the moment for you, hon, or were you looking forward to a more pompous affair?"

She gathered her wits, and tugging him to his feet, she threw her arms around his neck. "Yes, I'll marry you, Special Agent Luke Keltry." Releasing her hold around his neck, she held him at arm's length. "As for the right here, right now, are you intending to acquire this marriage license the way I think you are, by calling in a favor because of our help in the return of The Maiden of St. Marys?"

Luke grinned. "You know me so well."

She held up a finger to the minister, and pulled Luke farther away so as not to be heard. "If we do this now, we have a bit of a problem. I don't have any identification with my real name other than the IPA creds. I really don't think we should use those even if we could. But I'm pretty sure a picture ID is required along with a birth certificate."

"Agreed, but I believe we can get around that, as well, if the judge here allows us to use a fax machine and with the help of your *sisters* back home."

Rayla caught on, and in an instant realized this was exactly the sort of thing that defined her. Spur of the moment and somewhat reckless, not-well-thought-through decision-making blazed within her renegade spirit. How else could someone like her possibly enter into wedded bliss?

Scrunching her nose and biting her lower lip the way she knew Luke loved, she swung her gaze from him to the minister. "Can you give us an hour?"

32

LYING IN LUKE'S ARMS in the veritably comfortable king-size bed in their Cupola suite, having just consummated their marriage vows—several times—Rayla felt a contentment she had never before experienced. Odd. She had always considered her life one of ultimate contentment, but now she realized a key component had been missing.

This.

True love and commitment to one man—this man—for the rest of her life. She was flying high and so was Luke, she knew.

Procuring the marriage license from the judge at the courthouse proved easier than she'd imagined, once the man lost his grumpy attitude. The chief of police, the general manager of Grand Hotel, and one of the island's richest men and biggest supporters, Jaimeson Pinchot, all extending their substantial influence went a long way to make a seemingly impossible feat actually happen.

With the judge's agreement to accept faxed documents, Rayla contacted the Robin(s), who were still at Amy's, and enlisted their help in faxing her driver's license and birth certificate to the Mackinac County Courthouse on the island. Luke enlisted his parents' help in providing his birth certificate. The judge accepted the online application and signed off on the expedited issuance of the marriage license.

She and Luke returned to Grand Hotel to suit up more appropriately for the occasion. Since the hotel required dress apparel for many of their activities, Luke had brought a suit and tie and she a trendy, off-the-shoulder, ivory chiffon tulip dress with an asymmetrical hemline that Luke told her was most flattering for her long, slender legs.

Upon being informed of the impending wedding, the concierge at Grand enlisted half the hotel to provide flowers, a horse and carriage, hors d'oeuvres with champagne, and even a cake for the "reception." The general manager pitched in, too. After obtaining permission from the executive vice president of Grand Hotel, she opened the jewelry store, allowing them to buy their matching wedding rings. They settled on silver tungsten with black polished carbide centers. *Gorgeous.*

So it was that, with two laptops set up to look on—one in Santa Monica for all of the Robin(s) and one in Lewistown, Pennsylvania for Luke's mom and dad—Rayla Lynn Rousseau, aka, *Thief à la Femme* and third generation member of the Robin(s) of the Hood was joined in holy matrimony to FBI Special Agent Luke Daniel Keltry.

Upon reflection, Rayla realized she'd yet again managed to secure it all. Her wedding, like everything else in her life, flaunted her renegade spirit with the radical elopement, but still allowed her to wear a beautiful dress, arrive at the church in style, carry a bouquet, have all of the Robin(s) present, and even to celebrate afterward at Grand Hotel with a top-notch wedding reception.

Life was definitely good, and she knew as she was sure Luke did too, it would only get better ... and more interesting ... from this point on.

From the Author

If you enjoyed this book and/or the first two in the series, please consider leaving me reviews at Amazon, Goodreads, tacked onto public bulletin boards, in strangers' mailboxes, public restrooms … you know… *everywhere*, and please tell all your friends. I would truly appreciate your help spreading the word. It means so much in the world of publishing, and it only takes a few minutes!

Don't forget to check out our brother series:
Requisition For: A Thief < 1 - 8 > *and* **< Prequel One >** and watch for **< 9 > The Thief Within** on the docket!

Please feel free to email me. I'D LOVE TO HEAR FROM YOU!

www.jadevereaux.com
judy@jadevereaux.com

Acknowledgements

It is with great pleasure and excitement that I announce my partnership with **Cunning Thief Books**. I hope to have many more adventures with this publishing platform.

Gracious thanks once again to my awesome Cover Design Artist/Interior Formatter Jeffrey Kosh, JK Graphics. Working with me is not easy, but you are always patient, caring, and encouraging. I appreciate you more than I will ever be able to tell you. You are extraordinary at what you do, and even better when you do it for me!

Equally gracious thanks to my editor, Natalie G. Owens, Divas at Work Editing. Your editing skills, encouragement, and obvious care for me are greatly appreciated. Love you, hon.

Love once again to Patti, Tarry, Tami, Wendy, and Laura for your willingness to lend your names and to have become permanent Robin(s) of the Hood. Hope you think it's as fun being a thief … oops, I mean *pretending* to be a thief … as I do!

Thanks and love to our newest *Thief à la Femme* characters: Barb Sutherlin and Deb Sines. Barb, you make a fabulous "thief-turned-FBI agent" with just the right amount of "badass bitch and snarky chutzpah." Deb, your "FBI agent-moonlighting-as-a-thief" supplies refreshing comic relief. We appreciate a little bit of larceny in everyone! Thank you, ladies, for lending your names to become *Femme's* newest additions.

Extrême d'appréciation to Grand Hotel, Mackinac Island, Michigan, and especially to Grand's Official Resident Historian, Bob Tagatz, for the personal tour and all your hospitality. Everyone at Grand Hotel was amazing, and the tour breathtaking. It is my pleasure to have had this opportunity to create my fictional heists in your phenomenal hotel.

Beaucoup d'appréciation to the Mackinac Island Police Department, and specifically Linda Sorensen and Corporal Ken Hardy, for answering all my police-related questions and offering realistic scenarios for the department's response to theft-related incidents on the island. You two were wonderfully accommodating. Thank you so very much.

Love and very special thanks to my amazing husband. Mark, you are my everything, and don't think for a second I take for granted all that you do. Thank you for your encouragement, technical editing, monetary contributions, and all of the love you shower upon me daily. Love you, honey … forever!

For anything in this book that is good and admirable, TGBTG!

About the Author

J. A. Devereaux is passionate about the thief who isn't really a bad guy, guys like Alexander Mundy (It Takes a Thief); Neal Caffrey (White Collar); the "Leverage" crew; REQUISITION FOR: A THIEF's Gregg Hadyn, Niki Grey, and Jaelynn Madding; and *Thief à la Femme's* Rayla Rousseau. Such characters motivated her extensive knowledge of diamonds and her own thieving skills—strictly for research and writing purposes, of course! A long distance runner, former cross country coach, and former singer/songwriter, she resides with her husband in Jackson, Michigan.

www.jadevereaux.com
www.facebook.com/reqthiefseries
www.twitter.com/devereaux_ja

https://www.instagram.com/devereauxja
Email: judy@jadevereaux.com